Who Wants to
MARRY a MAMMA'S BOY
and other stories

A regular columnist in a national daily, **Manjula Pal** has won two prestigious story-writing contests and has also written a storybook for children in Hindi. She has done reporting for the different magazines of *Delhi Press* and worked as a research scientist at AIIMS, New Delhi. She is a Delhi-based grandmother.

She can be reached at manjula_06pal@yahoo.co.in

Who Wants to
MARRY a MAMMA'S BOY
and other stories

MANJULA PAL

RUPA

Published by
Rupa Publications India Pvt. Ltd 2019
7/16, Ansari Road, Daryaganj
New Delhi 110002

Sales centres:
Allahabad Bengaluru Chennai
Hyderabad Jaipur Kathmandu
Kolkata Mumbai

Copyright © Manjula Pal 2019

Grateful acknowledgement is made to the following
for permission to reprint copyright material:
Penguin Random House India for the story 'Love is Also a Compromise' from
Love Stories That Touched My Heart edited by Ravinder Singh.
Gargi Publishers for the story 'Who wants to marry a mamma's boy' from
The Notebook of Romance (Moonlit Matinee 3) edited by Gargi Sarkhel Bagchi.

This is a work of fiction. Names, characters, places and incidents are either the
product of the author's imagination or are used fictitiously, and any resemblance to
any actual persons, living or dead, events or locales is entirely coincidental.

All rights reserved.
No part of this publication may be reproduced, transmitted, or stored in a retrieval
system, in any form or by any means, electronic, mechanical, photocopying,
recording or otherwise, without the prior permission of the publisher.

ISBN: 978-93-5333-591-5

10 9 8 7 6 5 4 3 2 1

The moral right of the author has been asserted.

Printed at HT Media Ltd, Gr. Noida

This book is sold subject to the condition that it shall not,
by way of trade or otherwise, be lent, resold, hired out, or otherwise circulated,
without the publisher's prior consent, in any form of binding or cover
other than that in which it is published.

*To my husband Ashok,
our children—Surabhi and Vivek,
and our grandchildren—Manya, Divyank,
Abhinav and Aryan*

With Much Love

Contents

Preface | ix

My First Love Affair | 1

Who Wants to Marry a Mamma's Boy? | 16

Dear Shalini | 27

Virgin @ Forty | 43

Love is Also a Compromise | 57

When Krishna Came to My House | 68

The Koh-i-Noor Belongs to Me | 80

The Honey Trap? | 97

Acknowledgments | 117

Preface

The urge to write to express myself has always been there, since I was a teenager. I had the opportunity to do some feature writing for several publications and even wrote a children's story book in Hindi. However, writing as a serious occupation happened only after midlife crisis hit me.

The short stories in this book have been written over a period of three decades. The story 'My First Love Affair' was written before the advent of electronic communication. It showcases the warp and weft of the social fabric of the time. The tales, 'Who Wants to Marry a Mamma's Boy?' and 'Love is Also a Compromise' won critical acclaim and awards. The final two stories 'Kohinoor Belongs to Me' and

'The Honey Trap?' deal with contemporary relationship issues.

I have captured the emotional journey of women through their different stages in life.

From a sixteen-year-old girl's experience with first flush of love, and her eagerness to explore the untrodden world of romance, to the dilemma of a career woman, caught between her work demands and her love life, and then finally succumbing to the compromises and commitments in her married life, and the likes reflect the range of themes in my stories. I have tried to lay threadbare the dynamics of fragmented relationships vis-à-vis rising individualism with a special emphasis on romantic bonds. It is for everyone to see that with continuous growth in hedonistic culture, lesser and lesser space is left for moralistic values in the society at large.

As a journalist, I am trained to look at things dispassionately often compromising with my sensibilities, but as a fiction writer, I have taken the liberty to let my imagination run amok, and bring to my readers the untapped areas of romance and relationships.

My First Love Affair

It was midnight when I took my second tablet of calmpose. It didn't help me either, as I was still not able to sleep. I heard the low, rhythmic snoring of my husband, sleeping next to me. I quietly slipped out of bed, lest I woke him up and went to another room. This pattern was not unique to that night only; the insomnia had been bothering me for quite some time.

The bug of the mid-life crisis, a 'cliché' modern-day syndrome, had bitten me. It had, in fact, started overpowering me. I knew that my two teenage sons didn't need me the way they used to. My husband, either busy or preoccupied, had mastered the art of how to remain indifferent to my mental turmoil. I was compelled to live a lonely life—aimless, nothing much to do, frustrated, moving from one room to another like a ghost. It was bugging me to no end. Utterly confused, I would introspect often: Where did I go wrong? Did I really end up with this drudgery of a life out of my own foolishness?

In my case, I realized that leaving my lucrative job after I got married was a mistake. I was the only one responsible for my present situation and I had begun to think of myself as a martyr who had sacrificed her promising career in the service of her family to become a full-time homemaker. When I looked at my college mates doing well in their careers, I would feel envious of them. I could have been like them and not felt wasted and so small in my own eyes.

How I wish I hadn't been swayed by my husband's advice to leave my job after the marriage, or that I had treated my mother-in-law with more compassion and respect so that she would have stayed with us and not opted to live separately. I failed on that score too. After all, so many working women are able to organize a support system that takes good care of their children.

In one's late forties, what choices does one really have if one wishes to start afresh in any profession? I decided to reorganize myself, lest I go crazy or slip into depression. I

My First Love Affair

thought of taking my situation on as a challenge and started probing avenues, which could give me an occupation along with satisfaction.

To start my next innings, I looked for my certificates and academic records that were relegated to storage ever since I got married over two decades ago. It had been dumped in a small bag that was kept in the loft. It had come as part of my dowry, but was never opened till date.

The bag was taken out from the loft and opened. Besides academic records, there were some other interesting things too that I had completely forgotten about. The most important object that caught my fancy was a partially written diary, from my college days, with no mention of dates.

It was not a proper diary in the sense that it was not an expensive, intricately bound notebook but a regular textbook copy with an ordinary cover. In addition, there were some loose, scribbled chits, some written in my handwriting and some written by someone other than me, and a notepad.

I picked the diary and opened the first page. There was a poem written by me, in neat handwriting. I would like to share it with my readers, with a disclaimer that it was a teenager's amateur effort, who knew nothing about poetry writing.

When I was sixteen, my eyes met with a pair of eyes,
Tender, moist and beautiful,
They looked at me from top to toe and back into my eyes.
Our glances intertwined in a soft embrace,
I gasped, I choked.
Drenched in showers of emotions
Was it love? Love at first sight?
As I looked myself in the mirror,
I was embarrassed to find
that I was beautiful, that I was desirable.

Meenu

Reading it made me feel immensely nostalgic. Did I really write it? It looked so alien. I had totally forgotten about the whole affair. Moreover, poetry writing had never been my forte, and this piece could be just a spillover of emotions.

I had found an occupation—my start-up project as a writer. I decided to declassify the whole text, secretly kept under lock and key, everything that was written in the diary and on the loose chits. I was greatly amused and equally thrilled to peep into the life of an innocent young girl and her experience of first love.

I would have to confess that the subject appeared so different from the me of today that the whole exercise appeared like I was becoming the biographer of my own life story.

The first thing I did was overhaul my son's room. Ever since he had left to pursue his graduation at a university abroad, it had been lying unused. I changed my 'workplace' to my taste. All the weird posters were pulled off. The multicoloured paint on the walls was removed to a broken, white monochrome. My desktop, as I was still uncomfortable with a laptop, was fixed on the study table. My passion for music was gratified with my favourite music system fixed in place. Some old-style furniture and a reclining chair were all that adorned my new 'karmabhoomi'.

The story goes back to the sixties and seventies, a time when the atmosphere in schools and colleges was very different from today. It was quite old-fashioned, and all the more conservative in the towns of UP where my father was posted.

The majority of schools used to be either all girls or all boys. However, the graduate course at the University of Allahabad was coed, where I joined as a science student. Even though boys and girls would study together, intermingling and openly moving around with each other, even in mixed groups, was frowned upon. If a boy and a girl were seen in each other's company too often, it was considered inappropriate—even scandalous. In the classrooms too, the first couple of rows, depending upon the number of girl students, were reserved for girls.

In my pages there was a vivid description of an incident written in great detail. After the admission process ended and before the beginning of the regular classes, I saw a very good-looking boy about my age standing in the guestroom in my house. It was morning. We looked at each other, without exchanging a word, just looking at each other for some time. After a while, I went inside and asked mother about him.

I was told that he was the son of my father's friend, who had also been admitted for the science course at the university. He was in his pyjamas, which meant that he had come the previous night after I had gone to sleep. He was in the engineering group while I was in the biology group. He was putting up in the hostel, but was living with us for a few days to escape the dreaded ragging menace. His name was Manav.

Manav and I became friends. There was an instant chemistry between us. We would go to university together.

My First Love Affair

Classes had not begun so we spent time loitering inside the campus, exchanging glances with each other, intermittently.

We went to take a round of the biology department and then his engineering department. He noted down both the timetables pinned on the notice boards. I was greatly amused to find that the particular notepad on which the timetables were scribbled in his handwriting was kept in my forgotten trove.

He stayed with us for about a week or ten days, and then left for his hostel. We did not meet often after that, as we were in different departments and classes had begun, keeping us busy. This short acquaintance had changed me completely. I had developed a crush on him. He was constantly on my mind. The poetry-writing incident might have taken place at that time.

When I did not see him for a couple of days, I started missing him. There were no electronic communication systems in those days, so contacting him was a problem. Our departments were also not close to each other. One month passed and he had not come to see me. What if he had forgotten me? Was it a one-sided infatuation? I would be plagued by such thoughts. Finally, he came to see me and explained that he had not been able to find the time because his studies had commenced in full swing.

When a chance presented itself, I manoeuvred things so that I would be able to meet him more often. For BSc students, there were two hobby courses available in the university—German language and photography, out of which students could opt for one. He took the language option. Although I had no interest in learning German, and I still regret my decision of not opting for photography, I took it only to be with him. However, within a month, he declared that he was quitting German as his studies were suffering. I, too, left.

Luckily, we did not stop meeting off and on, in the university. We had learnt to manage our low-key affair along with our studies.

Our conversation was mainly restricted to books. Like the other girls of my generation, I would go for fiction, both in English and Hindi. Surprisingly, he had unique tastes. For the first time in my life, I had actually met someone who enjoyed reading the Oxford dictionary in his spare time. He would read a few pages slowly, word by word, and then flag it with a bookmark. He picked up where he had left off when he found time to read. I was shocked to learn that he had already finished reading the whole dictionary once. A nerd of course, I thought, but an adorable one.

On my part, I would sometimes discuss characters like Paro from *Devdas* or Lalita from *Parineeta* and Jane Eyre or

My First Love Affair

Tess. He would listen with a lot of interest. When I told him that I found Tess as pious as Sita, he was surprised by the idea of an English fictional character resembling the divine Sita.

He never read any fiction, though would unfailingly read the newspaper, which was rather uncommon in those days among boys of his age. He was very different from my cousins—much more mature and knowledgeable for his age. Maybe that was the quality in him that I fell for.

Soon, before I knew it, a year had gone by. Both of us did very well in our first year exams. I even topped my class.

During the summer vacation, my father was transferred to Delhi and I had to move into the girl's hostel to complete my degree. That one year of living in a hostel was the most pleasurable and memorable year for me. Manav had changed from being reserved to become more open and friendly. We had started meeting very often. He would come to visit me every other day. We would talk incessantly, giggle loudly and sometimes, even go for a stroll outside the campus.

On one of those days, he offered to take me for a movie. I happily agreed. Inside the theatre, when it was dark, he held my hand, lightly pressing it. In response, I squeezed back. Encouraged, he pulled my hand and softly kissed the back of my hand. It was my first experience of a romantic physical encounter. I was thrilled. When the lights came back on, we kept holding hands even when we returned to the campus.

After I reached my hostel room, I caressed the back of my hand which he had kissed and pressed my lips on the same spot. The sensation was akin to as if we kissed each other's lips. This incident was written in broken sentences, as if, indicative of pleasure combined with a sense of hidden guilt.

Somehow, after the movie incident, our conversation shifted to romantic sweet nothings from boring academics.

This romantic interlude made my life blissful—all honey and roses. I was often seen smiling, blushing most of the time, as was noticed by my friends. My studies became secondary to my love life.

Another interesting incident that was mentioned in the diary was the time I was afflicted with viral fever and got admitted to a small, four-bedded, healthcare centre on the hostel premises. The nurse came and told me that a boy, calling himself my cousin, wanted to see me, but he wasn't allowed inside for fear of infection. The nurse handed over a letter he had given her to give me and kept a glass of something on the side table next to the bed. It read: 'I wanted to see you, but she is not allowing me. Sending mosambi juice. Please drink it and get well soon'. I asked for a piece of paper from the nurse and replied: 'I too am dying to see you. Hopefully, I will get discharged tomorrow. Thank you for the juice. Don't worry, I am all right.' The nurse passed on my note to him.

I was touched to find that the note which he had written in his handwriting was also there along with other things I had been loath to discard.

Life was heavenly, time was flying. But as they say, all good things have to come to an end. The date of our final-year examination was announced, and the time to depart was nearing. Our minds were in a mess of confusion.

What would be our course of action after we finished our exams and went away to different places? Was it the beginning of the end of our love affair or was it possible to continue?

The possibility of a future togetherness appeared slim, as Manav had at least five to seven years before he would be able to settle down, and I knew waiting was not possible in my case. My parents wouldn't wait that long for me to get married.

I needed a commitment. Would he do that? On the other hand, there were my own feelings and my family to consider. I wasn't sure about myself and the reaction of my family. Considering all these roadblocks, we decided to part amicably, before things got out of control and we foolishly indulged in any activity that would make us ashamed or feel guilty. As we bid each other goodbye, we hugged each other tightly. We both had tears in our eyes. We touched each other's eyes to wipe off our tears.

Finally, with heavy hearts, we made a resolution that we wouldn't see or contact each other, come what may. As luck would have it, he was much stronger than me. He avoided me and did not break the promise even once. However, it was not easy for me. I got depressed beyond comprehension. I dreaded my decision of not meeting him. It affected my studies. I had done very well in the first year, but my grades substantially went down in the finals, whereas Manav's grades were as good as ever.

Exams over, it was time to pack our bags to go home. I gathered courage and decided to express my feelings before we parted ways. I was able to send a message through someone, wanting to see him one last time. When he came to the appointed spot, I told him about my intense love for him and my desire to stay committed to him till we could marry. I told him of my resolve that I would wait for him as long as needed for him to settle down.

Contrary to my expectations, he looked perplexed. He held my hands, kissed them and patted my cheeks, said nothing and went away.

It was a big let-down for me. I was ashamed of myself for behaving like that. It was not easy for me to forget my humiliation. I was low on self-esteem. I was sorry for the stupidity shown on my part.

My First Love Affair

My train ticket was bought. It was time to go to the railway station. I was sitting at my reserved window seat. Just before the train was to start, I saw him approaching me. He handed over an envelope. 'Please read the letter inside and forgive me,' he said, giving me an affectionate look and before I could react, went away.

I found that the letter was kept nicely folded between the pages of the diary. I took it out and began reading:

My dearest,

When I think of our friendship, believe me, I cherish it. I will always hold you in the highest esteem. At my age, what matters is my career and only my career. Everything else is secondary. I am very focused on that. I loved talking to you and spending time with you. Whenever I was tired of studying and wanted to de-stress, I would head to your place. I admit I was happiest in your company. You were always a source of inspiration to me and I always felt rejuvenated after meeting you. I like you and respect you. If I have been misinterpreted in any other way, please forgive me. I wish you only the best in life.

Yours sincerely,
Manav

This letter was like a slap on my face and my ego. But it helped me in getting over my idiotic crush. I headed home in near-normal state of mind.

I concentrated on my future plan of action. From biology, I switched to learning computer courses, the emerging field of knowledge that offered ample job opportunities.

A few years passed by. Manav, by then, was history to me. I got employed and was happy with my life. In the meantime, my father had started looking for a suitable match for me. In those days, a career was not considered a priority over matrimony for daughters.

Then something unimaginable happened. After a gap of nearly three years since Manav and I had last met, my father got a letter from him, asking for my hand in marriage, with only one condition—that we would have to wait for at least one or two years till he got settled in a job. Papa gave me the letter and assured me that I could take as much time as I wanted to decide. He even promised to abide by my decision, and in case I chose to say yes, he would talk to Manav's parents.

I took the letter, read it again and again. This was my time to express my disdain. I refused and explained that there was nothing between us. He was free to choose a match for me.

Now, sitting in my converted work space reading all these

papers, I was reminded of my decades-old love affair that I had completely forgotten. It was like I was looking at a young girl objectively, and she was encountering unsurmountable hurdles in the way of her love affair, with all her pleasure and pain.

Teenage romance is like a dewdrop—pure, magnificent, surreal, and at the same time, so frail, transient and vulnerable that it cannot withstand the slightest vagaries of nature and like a dewdrop it evaporates with the first kiss of the rays of the Sun.

However, at the same time, like in my case, there must have been something permanent in that forgotten affair. Otherwise what was it that had stopped me from destroying the memories that were secretly kept like a treasure for so long? At the end of the day, I realized that your first love doesn't die down so easily. It always stays somewhere inside you like a tiny tattoo near your heart that can be forgotten sometimes but can never be expunged permanently.

Who Wants to Marry a Mamma's Boy?

It was a usual Sunday morning in Raghav's household, with no particular agenda for the day. Just as he was having his energy drink after a workout on the treadmill, his wife, Meera, called him to attend a phone call from his friend, Amrit, on the landline. Raghav got up to take the call, as he mostly kept his mobile switched off at night. Amrit wanted to discuss a serious matter regarding his girlfriend and himself and desired to come over right away. Raghav okayed the plan and told Meera about the call.

'Shall I arrange for some stuffed "mooli gobhi" parathas

with curd, instead of the regular toast and eggs, in case he is having his breakfast here?' she asked.

'I think I would rather take him out, so that we can talk freely and undisturbed, as he was sounding really very upset,' replied Raghav.

Meera looked relieved and started playing with their one-year-old daughter.

Raghav and Amrit were old pals from their college days. They were always there for each other in need, and could discuss anything under the Sun without censoring anything or being unduly judgemental.

For the last three years, since Raghav's wedding, Amrit had another reason to become Raghav's family friend because during that occasion he had met his future girlfriend, Tarang, who was Meera's cousin. It was like love at first sight for him and it made him try out every possible antic to woo her and ultimately succeeded in getting her attention.

Amongst the entire young female crowd present in the ceremony, Tarang definitely looked the prettiest. Fair-skinned with a nice figure and expressive eyes, she looked radiant in an electric blue anarkali. Amidst the 'who is she, who is she' whispers, Meera introduced her as her cousin to Raghav's friends. Tarang was on the verge of completing her MBA back then.

Not very long after his marriage, Raghav learnt that Amrit and Tarang were dating each other and were often seen moving around together, hand in hand at various places. Amrit, with his good looks and great sense of humour, had always had his way with girls, right from his school days, and hence the story of their mutual admiration did not come as a surprise. They looked very much in love and fabulously picture perfect as a couple. After passing out from their respective colleges, they started their careers in different corporate sectors.

Raghav took Amrit to the Delhi Gymkhana club and occupied a corner table away from the public view. He tried his level best to make his friend comfortable and ordered a regular continental breakfast for the two of them.

Without beating about the bush, Amrit poured his heart out. He said that he was having second thoughts and had many reservations regarding marrying Tarang. There were many issues which were forcing him to think twice. He confessed that it was not an impulsive decision, but after months of serious deliberation that he had reached that conclusion.

At his friend's outburst, Raghav was surprised and greatly confused. Was he the same person who just a year back, would blush at the mere mention of Tarang's name, totally smitten by her charm, head over heels in love with her? He was not convinced.

'Are you hiding something from me, I mean, are you seeing someone else?' 'Me?' asked Amrit, and added, 'No, no. Nothing like that. In fact neither she nor I are seeing anyone else. It is due to the difference in our attitudes towards life, our perspectives regarding happiness. Moreover, our value systems are also very dissimilar. I think that we are two different people, not compatible and not made for each other as husband and wife.'

He paused for some time as if looking for words to explain his point of view.

'You see, Tarang is very ambitious and pursues her job with a passion. Her priority in life is her career more than anything else, including her family. For me, a stable family life is very important, which is not possible with a full-time, ambitious working woman.'

'So what? After all, she has invested so much in life to achieve this position; she deserves what she has got. You sound too orthodox, like a male chauvinist.'

'But that does not mean she should disregard other responsibilities of her life. Previously we were seeing each other at regular intervals, but gradually, after she took up her job, she got very busy, so much so that she never had time to even talk to me for several days. We meet hardly once or twice in three to four months. See, we have shared beautiful moments together. We were in a serious relationship. What about our commitment? Sometimes I wonder if I at all occupy any space in her mind and in her life.'

'Maybe she needs her space with a very demanding job or it could be that she is taking you for granted.'

'Frankly speaking, I am feeling neglected and unwanted. Neither does she call me, nor does she respond to my missed calls. It seems like she is avoiding me. Recently, when I could not contact her for about two weeks, I got worried and upon enquiring from her office, I learnt that she had gone on a tour abroad for a month. She did not even care to inform me!'

'Did you not confront her as to why she behaved like that?'

'I did and like always, she said sorry and that it was the pressure of work and nothing else, and that she truly, truly loves me.'

'That's strange.'

'Yes, you are right. I have a feeling that it is not going to work out. A broken affair is better than a broken marriage, and I wish to avoid that calamity, which in all likelihood, is going to happen in the future in case we decide to marry. I am already thirty and she is just two years younger than me, yet she does not appear to be in any hurry for marriage. But I wish to settle down as early as possible.'

'What do you want me to do? I feel both of you should

talk it out without involving anyone else.'

'I really do not know how to put across my point of view to her; in fact, she has no idea about what is going on in my mind. Sometimes I wonder if she is really serious about me. I do not want to live in indecisiveness; therefore I need your help.'

They discussed in detail how they should go about it. Finally they decided to organize a meeting between all four of them—Amrit, Tarang, Meera and Raghav—to sit together and talk it out, explain everything that was bothering Amrit, without name calling, offending or provoking each other.

Thus a meeting was finally arranged. Meera dropped off her daughter at her parents' place and all four of them sat together at Raghav and Meera's residence.

Amrit, without mincing any words, straightaway told Tarang his apprehensions about their future life together. He also suggested that they seriously think about their marriage plan as to whether to go ahead with it or abandon it.

Tarang appeared shocked and went pale. She was dumbfounded.

Amrit took her hands in his, gave a pat on her shoulder and said, 'You are a nice girl. You have a very promising career and a bright future. In just two years' time, you have got a raise three times. You are travelling and seeing the world at such a young age. Most importantly, you love your job and have all the reason to be proud of your achievements.'

He paused for a while, had some water and proceeded, 'I too have a very challenging job. I often get my office work home. Because of the time difference, I work and attend conference calls from the US at all odd hours. In my kind of job, switching off when you come home is not possible. A house does not run when both husband and wife have such demanding schedules. Had I been in a more secure government job or had my own business, I could have managed. But I admit that I am not a multitasker. I cannot take care of the home along with my job and maybe a child in the future. Besides I cannot imagine you handling all the burdens alone.'

Tarang had by then regained her composure. She asked, 'Who is looking after all this now? What is the problem? You look after your career and I look after mine the way we do it now. With so much money at hand, there will be ample domestic help available.'

Amrit got irritated. 'My food, my wardrobe and everything is being looked after by my mother now and I don't have to bother about any of the household problems. Even you are living at a paying guest accommodation, having a 'dabbawala' to get your food. Such an arrangement cannot work in any household. Eating out once in a while is fine, but proper homecooked food is necessary for most of the days. Even if we have outside help, who would organize the functioning? Moreover, I have seen in my own home that outside help is not always dependable.'

Tarang was visibly angry and retorted, 'Aha, now the cat is out of the bag. Now I know; you are a typical mamma's boy. You refuse to grow up. You don't want to take any responsibility, therefore these silly arguments. With this attitude, you can't marry any working girl for sure, and please, mind you, I will marry any dud but never ever a mamma's boy.'

The atmosphere was getting heated up. Meera tried to cool Tarang down, but she refused to calm down. Her forehead and upper lip showed sweat drops. Raising the pitch of her voice, she got up and almost shouted at Amrit, 'In case you are indirectly hinting that I leave my job as a pre-condition for our marriage, I'm sorry, I refuse to marry you before you decide to dump me. And by any chance, are you jealous of my success?' With this, she walked out of the house. It was shocking for both Raghav and Meera, the way a beautiful affair had ended.

Amrit, however, had anticipated that reaction. He looked unmoved and calm and said, 'Didn't I tell you? I could foresee it happening and fortunately it happened before marriage and not after. Divorce is the last thing I would want. Why should I commit a mistake and then learn from it; instead, why not avoid committing it in the first place?'

'So what's next?' Raghav asked.

'I am going to ask my mother to look out for a girl for me. I don't have the time and energy for romance and affairs and frankly speaking I am done with it. And I am sure Tarang, who is a very strong girl, will forget all this and find a suitable partner soon. It is not fair on my part to keep her hanging. I understand that it will take some time for both of us to move on, but I am sure, ultimately things will be fine.'

Amrit's mother, Geetanjali, after hearing what had happened between her son and his girlfriend, got quite upset. She had met Tarang many times and had a liking for the girl. She suggested to Amrit to think over the matter more objectively. She argued that Tarang had a very promising career; therefore it was unfair to expect her to make compromises at a time when her career was at an early stage. She even blamed herself for being so indulgent in her son's upbringing, and promised to help them in the running of their household. Amrit refused to enter into any kind of argument with his mother and left the scene.

Geetanjali thought that the best thing to do was to give him some time and thus the topic was laid to rest.

With the passage of time, the fun-loving, outgoing and extroverted Amrit was becoming a recluse. His nonchalant behaviour, his morose looks, his reduced diet, etc. was worrying Geetanjali. Noticing all these changes in her son, she felt very sad and wanted to help but did not know how to handle him. Whenever she tried to discuss anything with him, he would get irritated and walk away. His parents feared that with his careless attitude, he might even lose his job.

'Should I talk to Tarang?' she asked once, hesitatingly.

'Please do not dare, otherwise I won't forgive you.'

'But you are not getting her out of your system. Life does not end there. Either you move on or sort things out with her.'

Raghav was also trying his best to cheer Amrit up and sometimes would take him out for a change. His argument was that whatever happened was the best for both of them and there was no need to sulk. He was not sure whether it was due to rejection or some kind of a subconscious guilt that Amrit was suffering.

Geetanjali had heard a lot about girls getting depressed after a break-up but her son was no different. She even thought of taking a counsellor's help, but Amrit got furious at the suggestion. It was a difficult task to get him out of his melancholic phase. She continued to look for girls in various matrimonial sites and also through word of mouth, but somehow Amrit was not taking much interest in the matter. A broken affair had transformed him beyond comprehension.

Nothing much changed in Geetanjali's house during the next couple of months. Then they came to know of something which was like a harbinger of good times for the family. They got the news through someone that Tarang had got married to the son of a business tycoon. The news was received very well by Amrit too as if he was relieved of a big burden. Geetanjali, as a mother, could foresee the change coming, but preferred not to confront him.

Amrit gradually started behaving his like his earlier normal self and even started taking part in the bride-hunting exercise with his mother. He was frank in admitting that an aggressive career was a 'no no' for his life partner, though he was not against a working girl with a less demanding job that allowed her time for the family also. His present state of euphoria intrigued Geetanjali in the same way that his erstwhile melancholy had. However, she was happy that her son had gotten over the Tarang chapter and had moved on in life with a positive attitude.

Dear Shalini

In traditional households, parents and guardians start thinking about settling their daughters down right after they finish their formal education. In my case also, after I finished my master's, my parents started worrying about my marriage. They kept enquiring time and again that if I had someone in mind already, then they would willingly go by my choice. But to their utter dismay, I went on denying it every time. Therefore, the arduous task of finding a match was left to them.

Arguments, debates and disagreements resulting in chaotic scenes were taking place on a regular basis in my house. On the one hand, according to my parents, my eligibility in the marriage market was going down by the day as I grew older, and on the other hand, rejections from either side—ours or the boys'—were happening very frequently.

Parents have become smart these days. They don't like to take all the responsibility upon themselves and so, they always take their daughters' consent before finalizing a match. God forbid, if anything were to go wrong later on, they could put part of the onus on the girl's shoulders. Thus, the final decision to choose my life partner among the available choices was left entirely to me.

At that time, Shalu Di proved to be a big succour. Dr Shalini Sharma was a professor in the department of social sciences at the university when I first met her as a student. Usually, after passing out, the student-teacher relationship ends, but that did not happen in our case. An age gap of nearly twenty years was gradually bridged and she became from Ma'am to Shalu Di. We had become good friends and would discuss anything under the Sun, including our personal lives.

I confided in her about the oppressive atmosphere in my house and how I was finding it difficult to take a decision. She advised me to ignore the nagging because it was coming from a place of concern and love for me. But at the same time, she told me not to act hastily. Marriage, after all, was a matter of great concern and should be taken very seriously, and not impulsively. She proved to be a great help in my decision-making exercise.

According to her, I should be open about my inclination and decide if I wanted to be a career girl. Frankly speaking, I was not particularly keen on the idea. I thought I would be happy as a homemaker provided there were no financial obligations.

Her important advice was that for a marriage to work one should look for similarities in nature, interests and intelligence rather than differences, made a lot of sense. Together, we scrutinized the options and were finally able to take a decision. I got married and remained, for a long while, a full-time homemaker—happy and content.

Seeing my affection and respect for Shalu Di and our involvement in each other's lives, my husband wanted to know more about her, both as a person and as a teacher.

I told him about her, beginning with the fact that there was a great disparity in the social status of Shalu Di's and her husband's families. While Mr Sharma came from a wealthy family, Shalu Di came from a middle class background. Theirs was a love marriage.

Mr Sharma was interested in philanthropic causes from a very young age, an uncommon trait usually not seen among youngsters. Shalu Di was doing a doctorate in social science and was working in a community. Their common interests and their resolve to do social work for the underprivileged was what brought them together.

Mr Sharma had opened a trust in which he would continue to deposit a fixed percentage of his earnings regularly. The trust was mainly engaged in helping accident victims. He had a registered helpline number that could be accessed round the clock. There was facility for an ambulance that would fetch the accident victim from any place, and then ferry him to the nearest hospital. The patients would receive immediate medical attendance, sometimes even free of cost in case they couldn't afford the cost of treatment.

As a matter of fact, the amount of money that was spent on the charitable work was much more than the obligatory, mandated corporate social responsibility.

Shalu Di would personally oversee the financial aspect of the trust, lest it landed in the wrong hands. The couple never bragged about their kindness and charity work, but tried to keep themselves away from the glare of the media as far as possible.

My husband was very impressed. He had heard about the

trust and its work, which was often publicized and praised in the media.

※

It was a pleasant surprise for us to receive an invitation on the occasion of Shalu Di and her husband's twenty-fifth wedding anniversary. My two small children were very happy to receive a big packet of Lindt chocolates that came along with the fancy invitation card. My husband was excited too, when I told him of the expected grandeur, excellent cuisine and elaborate bar. The foodie that he was, he was looking forward to the occasion.

The impressive venue was their large farmhouse and the party was on expected lines. My husband and children enjoyed everything to the hilt.

On our way back, he praised the couple for the respect and companionship they showed each other through their body language and behaviour. He wanted to know more about their charitable work that he found was quite unique in its nature.

I knew the background well; therefore I told him what I knew about them.

※

Shalu Di had told me about an incident that had taken place when Mr Sharma was a boy of fourteen. That incident, which I narrated to my husband, had changed the impressionable young boy's entire perspective towards life. While being driven to school in his car one fine day, Mr Sharma, then fourteen, met with an accident. The rider on the bike was killed on the spot, and his ten-year-old son sitting at the back was gravely injured. His driver stopped the car and called an ambulance for the deceased and his unconscious son. Later on, after dropping the junior Sharma home, the driver surrendered himself to the police.

The driver was booked for negligent driving and sentenced to six months. Mr Sharma, the father, taking the moral responsibility upon himself, heavily compensated and offered every kind of support possible to the victim's family and continued to look after the deceased's son's welfare, helping him complete his education and also ensuring that he was gainfully employed when he grew up. Their acquaintance remained till date, as they still treat him as part of their family.

The accident, at that time, proved to be so disturbing for the psyche of the child that it was a big turning point in the life of the very sensitive and emotional junior Sharma. So much so that his father had to arrange for a counsellor to help him through the traumatic incident. The treatment went on for an entire year. He had even stopped going to his school for a long period of time and thus missed out on a year of schooling.

At that young age, he took a vow—when he grew up and started his own business, he would do whatever he could to help the accident victims, morally, physically and financially.

My husband was impressed but at the same time, was surprised to learn the reaction of a young fourteen-year-old boy. According to him, it appeared to be 'overboard'. Seeing death at such close quarters could be very traumatizing and psychologically devastating for an impressionable boy, but usually children outgrow the negative impression with time.

Moreover, drivers of rich people are often charged for their negligent driving and owners paying for their mishap are common occurrences, and the provisional six months sentence as in this case also, in all probability, would have been a bailable one.

While we were discussing the rationale of such exaggerated behaviour, I was reminded of one of the lectures in our class, when Dr Shalini was teaching the topic of altruism and various aspects related to it. Modern-day psychologists hold that the willingness to help is both self-serving and governed by selflessness. Therefore, altruistic behaviour benefits both, the giver and the receiver. It is nothing but the sensitivity of the person and how he reacts in a given situation.

I went on to elaborate. The professor once discussed in detail whether any kind of altruism could really be called a selfless act. She had cited an interesting example of American president Abraham Lincoln to prove her point. Once, while he was travelling with his friend, he saw some piglets drowning in a marshy pond. He stopped his carriage, lifted the piglets out of the pond and placed them in a safe, dry spot. Later on, he went on to explain to his friend that his act was not so much for the safety of piglets only, but for his own solace as well. If he hadn't done anything, he would have felt distressed the whole day spent in questioning himself about why he didn't rescue the piglets when it was so easy for him to do so. Helping others also increases one's sense of self-esteem. Maybe this was the case with Mr Sharma as well.

With the passage of time, after completing his education, Mr Sharma got engaged in his father's business. During the course of his planning for this ambitious project of social work, he met his love, Shalu Di, found her intelligent, gentle and caring, and both of them got married.

Months and years passed by. I learnt that Shalu Di had taken a sabbatical, since her husband was not keeping too well. His heart condition was of great concern to her, though not critical. We were in touch all the time and frequently exchanged notes and talked about our families at length, off and on.

By this time, both of Shalu Di's sons were married and all of them were living together in a joint family and together, looking after their common business.

On a fateful day, while I was sitting with the newspaper and my morning cup of tea, I noticed an obituary that saddened me. It was about Mr Sharma's demise. From my calculations, he had passed away about fifteen years after they had celebrated their twenty-fifth marriage anniversary. I gave the bad news to my husband. He was saddened too. Shalu Di had been telling me of his ill health, but that the end would come so soon was not expected.

We went to the crematorium on the second day. It had not been possible to have a personal interaction on any of those days. I thought I would visit her later after the guests had gone and things got back to some sense of normalcy.

A month passed, and while I was still thinking about a suitable time to pay Shalu Di a visit, I received a call from her. She expressed her desire to spend some time with me alone, just two of us together.

I went to her place. She was living in her personal suite, where she used to live with her husband. Her two sons were living in the same compound in their separate suites. They tried to meet every day for dinner, a custom Mr Sharma had initiated and was followed even after his death.

She appeared composed as she spoke about her husband's heart ailment, the surgeries and the fact that the end was sudden, but painless—a saint's death, as they say.

She told me of her loneliness and her plan to rejoin the college after a long sabbatical, to complete the last year before her retirement.

※

After dispensing with the formalities, she told me that she had called me over for a very personal matter, an important issue that she wanted to share with me and with no one else in the world.

She got up, brought an envelope and handed it to me. There was a letter inside. She wanted me to open it and read it. She declared that she found it accidentally two days back, in her husband's almirah while she was sorting out his things.

The contents of the letter she found were disturbing, so she wanted to share them with a person close to her and at the same time not unduly judgemental. She had called me her confidante.

On the cover of the envelop was written, 'To my beloved Shini', she asked me to take out the letter and read it. I felt hesitant, like I was infringing on her privacy. But I read it at her insistence.

My dearest, my very own Shini,

I know my end is near. Doctors give false hopes; it's their job. But I don't believe them. There is a secret of my life that I want to share with you. I could have done it much earlier, but for certain reasons, I wanted you to know only after I am gone. It was getting difficult for me to find time to write this, because you were always there by my side, never wanting to leave me alone. But today, fortunately, you had to go to visit your doctor for your routine check-up, which, against your insistence to postpone, I forced you to go to. I am taking this opportunity to write this letter that I have been contemplating for a long, long time now.

You know of the terrible accident in my childhood, the one that disturbed me and changed my life completely. I have told you about it in detail, not once, but many times.

I want to make a confession to you—I have been telling a lie all this time. The fact of the matter is that at the time of accident, it was me at the wheel and not the driver, as has been told to everyone. I was crazy to learn to drive and was coaxing my driver to teach me on the sly without telling anyone in the house. The street was more or less empty but out of nowhere, a pillion rider with a child sitting at the back and riding at a very high speed came in front of the car and collided with it.

After the accident, our driver swiftly lifted me and put me on the passenger seat. He sat on the driver's seat and looked around. The street was empty and he acted so fast that there was no witness to challenge the charge that the driver was not speeding at the time of the accident, and in fact, an underage boy had been driving.

The pillion rider was dead and his son was unconscious and gravely injured. My driver called for an ambulance. We waited till the ambulance arrived. After seeing them be taken away to the hospital, our driver left me home and surrendered himself to the police.

By taking all the blame upon himself, our driver saved our family from a lot of trouble. His benevolence stirred me, and I firmly believed that no amount of money could compensate what he did for us. I remember what my father had said in a fit of rage, that, but for him, you are at home, otherwise the juvenile justice board would have sent you to a correction home for God knows how much time.

There were only three persons, my parents and me—other than the driver—who knew the truth. It was the nobility of our driver that stopped us from telling even his family about the incident; otherwise, his wife would have blown up the case out of proportion. It is understood that the driver's family was adequately compensated and he was bailed out before his term.

I want to confess to you that ever since, I have been living with a feeling of guilt and it is only due to that guilt, which never leaves me, and I feel miserable at times. By helping accident victims, I feel I am lessening my remorse. I am not doing charity for anyone but self-service to give me peace and solace.

Shini, I did not tell you before because you love me so much that you would have taken the guilt upon yourself and suffered with me, which I did not wish to happen.

The reason for telling you now is that I do not want to die with this guilt on my soul. I feel unburdened now. I can now die in peace. I am feeling very light, as if, after telling you the truth, I am freed of the guilt that I bore for all these years. Please forgive me.

I know you will take care of the trust to whose cause both us have toiled so much. I leave it to you whether you want to tell my secret to our children or not.'

Yours, truly

As I finished reading the letter, I was choked with emotion. Tears started rolling down.

She spoke in a sombre tone, 'You know, guilt is the most

intense and painful emotion. Insensitive people deliberately try to expunge it from their system and memory, but the sensitive ones live with it. My husband did just that. I wish he had shared it with me while he was alive. I would have counselled him and helped him ward off his guilt in his lifetime itself. The accident was preordained, the result of an innocent mistake, and not an intentionally executed crime.

"The reason for his passion for philanthropy was due to his sensitive nature and his immense ability to empathize with people in distress. The incident was like a trigger. In all probability, if not for this incident, he would have found something else, or some other excuse to dedicate his life in the service of the needy. It was imminent. These are qualities that make some people great and distinct from others.

'Now what do you suggest? Should I or should I not tell my children about it?'

'Shalu Di, since you have asked for my opinion, I request you not to tell it to anyone, not even to your children. Let them revere him as a great human being who could not have committed any crime in his life. And frankly speaking, he never committed any crime. He was innocent.

'Further, your husband is dead and consigned to flames. Likewise, this document, his confession, should also be consigned to the flames. Try to forget it. Remember only his good deeds, which are abundant and attested to by the numerous thank you notes and messages from a number of people whose lives were saved due to his charitable trust.'

I hugged her and made her sit close to me.

I picked up one of the coffee mugs out of which we had taken our coffee a while ago, washed it, wiped it clean with a tissue paper and kept it in front of us. I crumpled the letter, put it inside the mug, lit a match stick and slipped it inside. The letter started to burn slowly.

She clung to me like my teenage daughter would. Both of us began to stare intently at the coffee mug, till the paper inside had turned into a pinch of cold, grey ash.

Virgin @ Forty

'Hello! This is regarding a matrimonial ad in the Sunday paper, am I right?'

'Yes, particulars are given. In case interested, kindly reciprocate and send yours.'

The advertisement was intended for Paridhi, a forty-year-old unmarried lady lecturer working at Delhi University. Her elder sister Megha, her only sibling, had given this ad in newspapers and various matrimonial websites.

Paridhi had been living with her parents in Delhi, while Megha was settled with her family in the US. Tragedy had struck at Paridhi's house when both her parents, first her mother and then her father, died within the span of one year.

Megha had come for the last rites after her father's death. She was deeply concerned about her younger sister's security and loneliness. However, Paridhi had no apprehensions living all alone and was coaxing her sister to not panic. The security system was in place and their cousins and their families were keeping in touch with her regularly, she tried to argue.

Megha, on the other hand, insisted that her sister must settle down and get married. Otherwise, she would never be able to live in peace so far away from Paridhi. She, in fact, had come with the intention of staying for a longer period of time, and wanted to see Paridhi nicely settled before she returned.

Before coming to Delhi, she had already done her homework to learn the usual protocol to be followed for fixing an arranged match. She was also conscious about what precautions should be taken in such cases, lest one gets duped, and so on.

To be on the safer side, Megha hired a private detective agency, which is a popular practice, to find the truth about the boy and his family, and to see whether it matched with the biodata given by the interested party or not.

After an arduous process of screening of many proposals, they realized that husband hunting was a tough job, more so for a forty-year-old woman. It is ironic that girls who like to settle down in their careers first often reach the age of thirty and before they realize it, they are closing in on forty, and are being branded as beyond the marriageable age. The same thing was happening with Paridhi as well.

Most of the matches were not even worth considering. Besides, many a time the information given in the biodata would not match with the details furnished by the detective agency. Misinformation and lying were rampant, and her age was also posing a big hurdle in the process.

After compromising on several points, they decided to interview one prospect. Dev was forty, educated, well-qualified, an issueless divorcee, was the only son heir to a a medium-scale business, owned a three-bedroom flat in Punjabi Bagh, and was living with his parents. The detectives had secretly found out that his yearly turnover was 50 per cent of what he had mentioned in his biodata, but even that was okay if other things were likable.

A meeting was arranged. Dev came alone. It took place in a congenial atmosphere. He was an above-average, good-looking man, had good mannerisms, was wearing a much-advertised, strong-smelling cologne and formal clothes. He looked to be the gymming kind, and had a good physique and no paunch—a big plus point for both the sisters.

Megha let her sister do the talking while she quietly and minutely watched the compatibility quotient between Dev and her sister. There was nothing odd in his behaviour, though it was evident that he was trying to show off by talking of big names and his association with them off and on.

During the course of the conversation, Dev asked, 'Paridhi, you are quite good-looking, and you're working as a permanent lecturer in a prestigious college, when most of the teaching staff is on an ad-hoc basis these days. How come you never decided to marry?'

He paused for some time and in the absence of a reply, thinking that he was probably being over-indulgent in the very first meeting, said, 'Just kidding.'

Paridhi got the hint, smiled and replied, 'Don't worry about it. My not marrying was not premeditated. It just happened. I do not have a boyfriend either. Maybe I never met anyone I liked enough.' After a pause, she continued, 'Could be because I studied in an all girls' college and now I'm teaching in a girls' college, I did not have too many opportunities to mix with boys. Our family is also conservative, not the outgoing type. Moreover, the last few years were hectic as I was attending to my parents' health issues along with the job.'

She looked at the attentive Dev and then went on to elaborate, 'Frankly speaking, I am very happy with my life. I love my job. I have my friends' circle, some of my cousins also live in Delhi and we keep meeting often, whenever there is an occasion, like a festival or marriage in the family. Up till now, I did not give a serious thought to marriage. It is only now, that too, because of my sister's insistence that I have agreed. She thinks that I must settle down, otherwise, she would not be able to live in peace in the US.'

Dev wanted to tell her about his story too, so he responded, 'I am single at the moment. I had an unfortunate divorce within a year of my marriage, about ten years back. I am little apprehensive about marrying again, so I want to take time and be very sure before I decide.'

'Fair enough. I appreciate your honesty. You may meet any number of times, but your marriage should be for keeps.' This time, it was Megha who answered.

They talked about his family and his interests, and also tried to indirectly probe into the reasons behind his divorce, although, they came a cropper.

The sisters discussed the proposal after Dev left and although they were not very happy with the match in the beginning, after having met him, decided to give it a try.

Next day, Dev got movie tickets for both the sisters, but Megha deliberately excused herself and let the two of them spend time with each other. Paridhi, on returning, appeared happy. She was comfortable in his company and thought him to be well behaved and a gentleman.

After a couple of meetings, it appeared that both of them liked each other. Until then, the sisters hadn't met Dev's parents. They expressed their desire to meet them so that the match could be formalized.

Finally, Dev suggested that he take Paridhi to his house to meet his parents. There wasn't any problem from the girls' side, since the match was more or less decided.

It was a Sunday. Dev picked Paridhi from her house and asked Megha to join them as well, but she wanted to give them time alone, so she made an excuse of an appointment with the dentist and suggested the two of them to proceed.

Dev took Paridhi to his house. Against his claim of a three-bedroom house, he had a two-bedroom flat on the first floor in the Punjabi Bagh area. His parents were not there. Paridhi felt awkward.

'My parents should be coming any time now,' he said and asked her to make herself comfortable in the drawing room.

'Would you care for a beer or a soft drink?' he asked her.

'A soft drink maybe,' Paridhi said. He took out a glass, poured a soft drink and gave it to her, and got himself a can of cold beer. He showed her some curios he had brought from a foreign tour. The price tags were not removed. It was clear that he was trying to impress her.

They talked about the décor and whatever changes she would like to make in the drawing room. 'From now on, you will be the lady of the house, as my mom is old and is eagerly waiting for me to get married and rid her of the household duties.' Then he added, 'You see, she is a simple, good-hearted lady. You will love her.'

Dev sat by her side, a little too close, and slowly and systematically started making advances towards her. Getting romantic and uttering a few sweet nothings, Dev gently encircled her shoulders with his left arm. He started to comb her hair with the fingers of his right hand, caressed her cheeks and suddenly, tilted her face towards his and planted a passionate kiss on her lips.

Paridhi was not feeling comfortable with his overtures. 'Please, don't. I am not ready.'

Dev, disregarding her squirming and her resentment, held her tight and started to massage her torso.

Paridhi tried to disengage herself. 'What are you doing? I understand we have almost decided to get married, but you must wait. Or are we not getting married? All this cannot happen before our marriage.'

Dev would not stop. His actions had surpassed her threshold of tolerance. He ignored her and his hand slipped down to her waist and the belt of her jeans.

Paridhi was seething with anger. She felt violated and pushed him hard off her with both her hands. Dev almost toppled on one side hitting his temple with the corner of the centre table.

Disgusted and humiliated, he got up, went inside and took some time to come out. He was smelling of Savlon, which he had possibly used to clean the bruise on his temple, and sat on the sofa kept opposite her.

Visibly irritated, he said, 'I don't understand. How could you reject me like this? I never expected you to be so naïve. I am totally confused. Virginity at this ripe age is not something to celebrate. It rather goes against your femininity.'

'I said in the beginning that I never had a boyfriend. Why? Don't you want your wife to be a virgin at the time of marriage?'

'In what era are you living? These days boys and even girls lose their virginity by their early or mid-twenties. Why should I expect a woman of forty to be a virgin?'

He paused for some moments, then asked, 'Tell me

frankly. Did you never think of getting close to a man? Never thought of having sex before? To me, it doesn't appear normal.'

Paridhi was dumbfounded.

After a short while, he again continued, 'Look, don't get me wrong, but in any marriage along with mental compatibility, physical compatibility is also very important. Therefore, before we decide to tie the knot, don't you think we should check out, whether we are compatible physically also? Like-er-in case…you're frigid?'

Paridhi was shocked at his humiliating, indecent proposal. She almost screamed, 'You are disgusting, you creep, and a liar! Where are your parents? You manipulated both, your parents and me into doing all this. I doubt whether you are even serious about marriage or you just want to have some fun. I can only hate you.'

That was the end of the Dev and Paridhi chapter.

There were many more disillusionments in the offing. The match-fixing exercise through the advertisements appeared non-productive, a total flop. The same was the case with matrimonial sites, where the number of proposals would be large but the information given was very different from reality. Arranged marriages were going out of fashion from the looks of it. Girls and boys were finding their mates themselves, either during college or at work. Girls who did not get attached to someone on their own would have to remain unmarried, maybe that was the case.

Megha, however, did not lose hope. She had something else in mind. A while back, a friend from the US had suggested a Delhi match—a 45-year-old widower, Alok, with two kids aged thirteen and five. She had rejected the proposal right away at that time, because she was not in favour of a widower with two kids for her unmarried, accomplished sister.

After some discussion, the two sisters, as a last resort, reluctantly decided to give it a try. After all, there was no harm in meeting once. First of all, she checked whether he was still available. After getting a positive response, they planned to meet.

The meeting took place in a club where Alok had a membership. The sisters found that Alok had a pleasant personality. He did not wear any flashy clothes or strong perfume and was dressed in casuals. He was well-mannered and articulate. He did not put any direct questions to Paridhi, but kept giving her coy looks. He kept on talking mostly to Megha about their common acquaintance abroad and on the changing weather patterns around the world.

After a while, Alok's driver brought a cute-looking little girl to the room and made her sit beside her father. She showed the adults around the table some chocolates she had bought and kept the glossy carry bag on the table.

She looked around and appeared very pleased to notice that she was the centre of everybody's attention.

A precocious child, she started the conversation, 'My school name is Parina but they call me Pari. Tell me, who is Paridhi Aunty out of you two?'

Everyone laughed. Paridhi pulled her by her hand and made her sit by her side. The child gave her a good look and proceeded, 'Papa has told me everything about you. I will tell about me. There is my dadi in our house and bhaiya comes during holidays. We drive once every month to Dehradun to meet him at the Doon School.'

After a slight pause, she asked Paridhi, 'Have you seen the Doon School?'

'No I have not been to Doon School.'

'Never mind, we will take you there some time. It is considered the best school ever.'

Pari paused for a minute, looked around, enjoying being attentively heard by the people sitting there, and with a serious expression on her face, continued, 'Paridhi Aunty, I should tell you one thing—that the decision of whether we accept you or not would be entirely mine. Okay?'

Alok looked visibly embarrassed and to divert attention, picked up a snack tray and started offering it to his guests.

Paridhi kept holding Pari's hand and whispered in her ears, 'Tell me, do you like me?'

'I do not know.'

Megha, avoiding precipitating the matter any further in a haste, tried to skip the topic and gestured to get up, making an excuse of another appointment.

While departing, Alok and Paridhi exchanged glances and smiled at each other affectionately and approvingly.

The two sisters had a long talk about every aspect of the match. Megha suggested that her sister should meet Alok alone without his daughter a few times, and also think very seriously, about whether she even wanted to marry a widowed father of two. According to her, it would mean a great deal of adjustment for Paridhi to suddenly become the mother of two pampered, perhaps even spoiled, kids.

Paridhi, on the other hand, didn't think she wanted to meet Alok alone. She expressed her satisfaction with the match. She was clear in her mind that in this particular case, if at all she went ahead, she would be marrying a family and not only the man.

She argued, 'Megha Di, let us be practical. Besides the security of a family, I am getting the full freedom to pursue my career the way I want to. Compatibility in any case would be a gamble; it has to be developed and nurtured. Honestly speaking, I have fallen in love.'

'So soon! What do you mean fallen in love? Without even knowing the man at all? Jokes apart, are you mad?'

'You misunderstand me. I'm not in love with the man, but with the cute little girl, Pari,' she said laughingly.

Megha didn't want her sister to act hastily. She thought Paridhi's decision was impulsive and tried to persuade her to meet Alok at least once more before making up her mind. But seeing her sister's consistent positive response, agreed, though reluctantly, with her point of view. She asked the detective agency to pack off, telling them that their job was not needed any more.

Alok and Paridhi exchanged vows in a simple ceremony in the civil court. Mission accomplished, Megha flew back to her home abroad.

A year has passed. Megha, along with her family are seated in a Delhi-bound flight, going to attend a function in Paridhi's house, to celebrate the arrival of her baby son. She shows posts to her family that were sent to her by Pari. There were some of Pari holding her small brother in her lap and some of the entire family. Megha breathed a sigh of relief and happiness.

Love is Also a Compromise

I was screening the medical records when I stumbled upon a file that caught my attention. It read:

Patient's name: Aditya Raj

Age: 62

Diagnosis: Tuberculosis

He had been registered in the hospital only a month back and was being given anti-tubercular treatment. I was confused. Who could this person be? Could it be him? The person I knew by this name had migrated to the US a long time back and we'd not been in touch for the past thirty years or so. This was during my new job in a private hospital—I'd recently taken it up post my retirement from a multinational. I was supposed to develop software that would facilitate displaying patients' complete data online.

Out of sheer curiosity, I took the address from his file and on the following weekend found myself standing in front of a DDA HIG (Delhi Development Authority, high income group) flat with his nameplate on the gate. A maid responded to the doorbell. She let me in. I saw a man sitting in an easy chair in the front room. He looked weak, unshaven and unkempt.

'Yes? Who is this?' he asked.

A thirty-year gap. Obviously, he had not recognized me. But it was indeed him. Disease had aged him beyond his years, but his trademark boyish grin was just the same. I decided not to disclose my identity. Using a fake name, I introduced myself as a social worker from the hospital, and said that I was filling a pro forma required for the follow-up of TB patients. Like any other lonely, elderly person, he appeared eager to talk—particularly to a woman—and he furnished me with all those personal details that were not really asked for.

He told me that he and his wife had returned to India about a decade back to take up a job in Delhi. He described in detail what happens when a loving life partner of many years dies. His wife had died a year ago, leaving him both physically and mentally drained. Thereafter, he'd neglected his health totally. It was during that time that he had contracted TB. His only son, a worthy one, was settled in the US, and had wanted Aditya to migrate there to live with him; but this had been delayed by one year owing to Aditya's medical treatment. He hoped to get completely cured of his disease while still in India. He might join his son afterwards so he said.

I felt sad and returned with a heavy heart. The last time I'd seen him was when we went to the airport to see him off.

My memory went into a flashback of the time when Aditya and I were classmates during our MBA days. Our friendship had slowly blossomed into a love affair. Fortunately, our parents also did not disapprove of our relationship.

After passing out, we got employed in two different companies in Delhi. While I liked my job, Aditya was dissatisfied in his. He changed his job at the first opportunity and went to Bombay.

Three years passed and my parents started insisting on marriage. However, Aditya was not prepared, because neither was he liking Bombay nor was he feeling settled in his second job. He also wanted to try his luck abroad. In fact, he had already fixed up with some company in the US and had decided to migrate. I did not seem to fit into his plans—at least for the time being. In any case, being the only child of my parents, I was not eager to migrate in a hurry.

Months before he was to leave for the US, he came back to Delhi, so that we could spend some quality time together. Our parents performed a small engagement ceremony. The process of getting my passport made was also initiated. After completing his formalities at the passport office, we went on a short pleasure trip to Shimla.

Merely a few days after he'd left, I learnt that he had given me the most unacceptable parting gift! I panicked and wanted to get rid of the unwanted burden as soon as possible. Thanks to liberal abortion laws, I got it done on the sly, without having to explain anything to the doctor. Half an hour's job at the hospital and two days of rest was good enough to get me back to my routine.

I decided not to tell anyone about my pregnancy, not even Aditya—firstly, because I did not want to bother him at that stage, and secondly, because I was the one who had actually messed up with the birth control pills and therefore felt solely responsible. No one, not even my mother, suspected anything. And I also forgot all about it afterwards.

In those days, international calls were very costly. Therefore, we stayed in touch with each other mainly through letters. But with the passage of time, I found that our demanding jobs and long working hours were slowly taking out much steam from our long-distance courtship. I had no choice but to wait for him till he got somewhat settled.

On the other hand, my professional life was good. With no responsibility, and with all the pampering from my parents, I was doing much better than many of my colleagues who had to look after their families along with their jobs. I was giving my hundred per cent to my work and was suitably rewarded too. I realized that once I married and went to the US, I would miss my job here. After all, the husband's job had to be given a priority.

It was at that time that we learnt through someone that Aditya had married. I clearly remember how, in complete disbelief, my parents and I went to his parent's house to enquire about the truth. It was not a rumour. He had indeed married an Indian-American girl. My father fumed at his apologetic parents and called their son's behaviour totally opportunistic and deceitful.

It was a big blow to all of us. For me the humiliation of rejection was much more than the loss of love. The unscrupulous fellow had dumped me without even giving me an explanation. I hated him! Even then, it took me some time to move on.

However, things gradually began to return to normal. My parents started looking for matches for me, but somehow, nothing worked out.

After facing disappointment in love, and with the kind of responses we received from proposals that my parents were negotiating, I felt extremely frustrated. I was also experiencing a change in my attitude towards life, particularly towards the institution of marriage. Widespread marital discord was apparent among my contemporaries, not only in arranged marriages but in love marriages too. I was alarmed by the increasing rate of divorces in my peer group—particularly amongst the so-called metrosexual couples. So, by that time, I became so disillusioned that I decided not to marry.

Frankly speaking, I was so busy with my job that I did not have any time to think about my single status. Moreover, I had no opportunity to mingle with men with whom I could have thought about marriage—some of the men I liked were already married while others were not the marrying type. My social life was limited to my parents and a selected few colleagues.

Years passed by. My parents' health was deteriorating. Frequent hospital trips—and the growing realization of living all alone when they were gone—depressed me.

While I still had five years of service left, both my parents passed away. Life was not the same after their demise. The loneliness was excruciating. Luckily, my habits of regular exercise and yoga kept me physically fit and mentally sane. During those days, I often thought of my unborn child and sometimes imagined caressing my baby in my arms. How I wish I had told Aditya about my pregnancy and forced him to marry me—not for anything else but for the sake of our child.

I retired in due course and thankfully, soon after my retirement, I got this hospital job, which I not only liked but which also kept me gainfully employed.

Then this Aditya episode happened.

I made it a point not to meet him when he visited his doctor next. But as the luck would have it, during his next monthly visit, he came looking for me in my room. Entering, he pulled a chair, sat down in front of me, looked into my eyes and called me by my name, 'Venu.'

I was shocked.

He laughed, 'I've done my homework well and know that there is no social worker in this hospital. I had a doubt, after you left my house, but it was not difficult to find out the truth. Why did you have to hide from me?'

Then he almost forced an invitation out of me. He announced that he would visit my house on the coming weekend and then left without even waiting for me to react.

He came as expected, but brought with him a big bouquet of flowers and a basket of fruits and other eatables. It was evident that he had taken special care to dress well. I was full of anger and pain, and got very irritated with his remorseless, aggressive attitude. He was like an intruder, not welcome in my house. I needed an explanation. Why did he ditch me in the first place? And now why had he stormed into my life? Stunned at his behaviour, I kept sitting rigidly, avoiding his glance.

All of a sudden he squatted on the floor in front of me, cupped my knees with his hands and put his head on my lap and started sobbing. 'I have wronged you. I am an offender. Still, I want to share the circumstances which forced me to behave like that. My job contract had expired and I was not getting an extension or another job. I was facing deportation. I hated to come back as a loser. I already had a marriage proposal from Ria, who was an American citizen of Indian origin. It was tough for me to decide. Besides, I could not see you marrying a person with such low self-esteem. I was not worthy of your hand, I thought. I became selfish and opted for the easier route. I married Ria to escape deportation. I could not muster the courage to talk to you directly, so I sent the news of my marriage through someone else... However, I could never imagine, even in my wildest dreams, that, you would remain unmarried. As for me, I was lucky to get a wife like Ria, who had a traditional Indian upbringing and was intelligent, loving and caring. I was blessed with a son and a happy married life.'

After he finished his explanation, he gently took my hands in his and said that he was ready to do anything and everything that would make me happy. He repeatedly begged to be forgiven. I did not respond. With tears in his eyes, he left.

He phoned me the next day and again expressed his wish to see me. I could not refuse. An opportunist he surely was, but he did not pretend. He was genuine, honest and transparent. I reasoned it out and forgave him. My long-lost love for him also started blooming. The big gap of thirty years was bridged before we could realize what was happening.

We started meeting often and even began going out together. Having a protective male escort by my side was flattering. I liked his exuberance and optimism. He used to look for excuses to pamper me. My heart pined for him in his absence. Our intimacy, however, was limited to holding hands and uttering sweet nothings to each other. He probably knew the limitations of his disease.

Our love affair was like that of two teenage virgins—restrained and yet eager to explore. We hardly quarrelled and never even argued the way we had in our youth. We believed in giving rather than demanding. In a way, our love was an untold compromise between the two of us. The feeling of belonging was beautiful and divine. Life was all honey and roses.

He was recovering well from his disease and had started gaining the weight he had lost. With his salt-and-pepper hair and boyish grin, he still looked handsome to me. I noticed that I too was getting compliments on my dressing sense and my good looks.

One day, after about a year of our memorable togetherness, he declared that he would not be seeing me for some time because his son was coming to wind up everything. Most likely, since he was fully cured of his disease, he would now go away with his son. I felt depressed. I took some time off from my job and stayed home to get over this low phase.

It struck me that he had used me again. I felt cheated.

After a couple of days, the unexpected happened. He was standing at my door.

'Sorry, I did not come before, because I was busy winding up,' he said.

'So you have come to say goodbye. When are you going?'

'I am not going anywhere, but I am going to shift into your house, as your house is better than my DDA flat, which I have already sold off.'

'Which means your son did not take you back with him and instead took away all your money?'

'No, that's not true. He wanted to take me along, but it was my decision not to go. And he did not take any money, because it has to be deposited in your account. I do not want to be living off you.'

'But why did you not tell me all this before?'

'Tell you what? Did you not see how madly in love I am with you? You silly girl, I need you more than you need me.'

He embraced me, with a hug that was tighter than ever before, and started passionately kissing me.

'Venu, I have the doctor's permission. I do not want to stop here.'

I did not mind it anyway.

When Krishna Came to My House

*D*elhi experienced its first monsoon showers. It came as a big relief after days of sweltering heat. It was evening. Streets that had been deserted were now abuzz with people coming out of their homes, seeking the fresh air, much relieved after their claustrophobic, air-conditioned confinement. The smoky smell of freshly picked soft corns roasting over charcoal and smeared with salt and lime, filled the air. Right from children to the adults, everyone was enjoying the roasted corn pods. The hawkers selling corns on pavements and on pulling carts were doing good business.

When Krishna Came to My House

My two children, my twelve-year-old daughter and six-year-old son were getting ready to come to the market with me to buy a few things. Suddenly, I heard the sound of a boy crying loudly, and intermittently shrieking. It seemed to be coming from outside the gate of my house. I asked my son to go out and see what the matter was.

When he returned, he told me that a small boy was crying as he stood next to his mother who was roasting and selling corns sitting on the pavement in front of our house. When I came out, I too saw the small child, about four years old, crying incessantly. I scolded the woman for not attending to her child.

She replied, 'This is not my child. He lives in the jhuggi adjacent to mine. His mother passed away only two days ago. He only has his father to take care of him. The father is an alcoholic. He has left the child with me and asked me to take care of him and assured me he would be back within an hour. Now 4 to 5 hours have passed. He must be lying in a gutter after getting drunk. I have to work here. I can't sit idle. The poor fellow has been crying a lot since his mother died.'

I took pity on the child and called him near me. He came sobbing. I brought him inside my house and requested my children to wait till I arranged to feed the child something. I then called my maid and asked her to get a glass of milk and make him drink the whole thing before I returned from the market.

At the market, I kept thinking of the poor child and his alcoholic father. Alcoholism has ruined so many lives. Poor women toil tirelessly to earn a living that will enable them to run their homes, paying for the daily dose of their husbands' addiction, only to be beaten as a reward. Why don't these wives leave their husbands and throw them out of their house, I often wondered? On the other hand, how easy it was for a husband to throw out his wife for any perceived 'wrong behaviour' on her part.

We returned home. On our way back, I enquired with the woman outside my gate whether the child's father had come back. 'No,' she said. 'I will soon be winding up and going home. Don't worry, I will take him with me.'

I looked at the child. He was soiled from the top of his head to the toes of his little feet. He must not have taken a bath since his mother had died. He was sitting quietly in a corner. I told the woman on the street not to bother about the child, as we would take care of him at least for today and would figure out what could be done tomorrow. I asked my maid to give him a good bath and went to pull out some of my son's old clothes.

After the bath and in clean clothes, the boy looked very different. He appeared to be a very charming, non-fussy and fairly disciplined child. He was the type who would get attention without asking for it. It was so easy to fall in love with that adorable child. If he had been born in a well-to-do family, he would have been spoiled rotten and doted on.

I asked him his name.

'Krishna,' he replied.

Krishna? Did he say Krishna? Suddenly something struck me. I gave him a good look. He had curly hair, doe eyes, chubby cheeks, petal-shaped lips and shiny skin. '*Oh my God!*' I thought to myself. I couldn't believe what I was seeing. He was an exact replica of the popular child god, Sri Krishna's. A photo print that we commonly see everywhere. I had a table calendar with different forms of Krishna printed on its leaves, including images of Him as a toddler, holding a flute, dancing with friends, riding a chariot, and so on. My eyes were fixed on the toddler print of Krishna and I was astonished to find the resemblance with this little boy, His namesake. The only missing thing was the headband with a small peacock feather at one side.

I am a devotee of God Krishna and became very emotional to see the similarity of features between the two. Was it possible that Bal Krishna himself was actually in my house? I was overwhelmed with the rather fanciful thought.

He looked straight into my eyes. I pulled his head near

my bosom. I could not let my gaze move away from him and kept on admiring his face.

Krishna disengaged himself, caressed my face with his tiny hands and said, 'Ma, you are like my ma who has gone to God to ask him to cure my father of his drinking habit. She will come back to me, after God grants her wish.'

I was touched. I kissed the child on his hands. I had already almost fallen in love with him. 'Your mother has asked me to take care of you till she comes back,' I replied.

He smiled.

I called my maid and instructed her to give him food and prepare whatever he wanted to eat and gave her a rug for him to sleep on.

Next morning, I told my family about the incident, and also about the uncanny resemblance of the child with the Bal Krishna print. My husband, children, everyone liked him and agreed with my decision that we would provide a house for the child till some proper, more permanent arrangements could be made. We also decided to send him to school and if need be, bring him up as best as we could, in case he ended up living with us forever.

As far as his father was concerned, we assumed he would be more than happy to be rid of the responsibility of bringing up Krishna. We would assure him of our good intentions and our decision to give him a secure environment. He could visit him whenever he wanted, but we decided that we would not leave the child with him.

Four days passed. Krishna was a no-nonsense child. He did not bother anyone. My son had given him a colouring book and some crayons. He would giggle often, paint and play with his toys. It seemed as if he had been living with us for a long time.

I had started seeing this child playing in our house, spreading happiness all over, as an incarnate of God. I imagined myself really blessed.

On the fifth day, I heard loud noises in front of our house. Someone was thumping the gate repeatedly. I opened and saw a sickly, dirty old fellow stinking heavily of liquor standing at the gate.

'Is Krishna living with you?' he shouted.

'Yes, he is with us. From now on, you don't have to worry about him. We have decided that he is going to live with us. As it is you cannot bring him up without his mother. So go away and don't shout,' my husband yelled at him.

He called his son. Krishna came and encircled my legs with both his hands. He looked scared.

'I do not want to come with you. I will come only when my mother will come to take me.'

'Don't worry. I will soon get a mother for you. You come

with me. They are not nice people. They will make you a servant and force you to work in the house. They won't even give you any salary and will even beat you.'

I was furious, 'Stop talking nonsense! How can a four-year-old child do household work? And when we are saying that we will send him to school, where does the question of making him work arise? Why don't you believe us? You can come and check it for yourself.'

'I have seen many cruel people like you. I don't trust you. I can leave my son only on one condition—that you give his salary to me every month,' he retorted.

My husband gave him a hundred-rupee note and asked him to come back again when he was sober.

He went away shouting that the amount of salary to be given he would fix.

It was clear that the man was not interested in keeping his child, but was intending to sell him. My husband did not want to get into any hassle with the human rights activists. We realized that it was not prudent to keep the child with us. We had to think of what could be done, what was best in the interest of the child.

The next day, we contacted the police, the childcare centres and the lawyers about such abandoned children and inquired into what could be done to secure their future. We were ready to give a stipend also. However, we did not get much help from the agencies, and therefore started looking for an orphanage ourselves.

After a lot of research, we found an orphanage that would keep him. It was run by a Christian missionary, so we decided to send him there, with a promise that we were allowed to call him to our place, whenever it would be convenient for us.

Krishna hugged me tightly when we were taking him to the shelter home. He didn't want to go away. We assured him that we would visit him frequently, and we were sending him only to stop his father taking him away from us.

He was quiet and very obediently went to the orphanage. He put up a brave front and did not cry.

The authorities suggested to us that we should not come to visit him before one week, or try to contact him else Krishna would find it difficult to adjust.

We went to meet him after a week. We were shocked by what we heard.

We were told that the father of the child had come the very next day and had forcefully taken the child away with him, with a promise that he would return him the day after, which never happened. I was angry at the sister in charge. They were strictly forbidden to hand over the child to his alcoholic father, why did they allow it?

❧

There was no way of finding the boy. I started looking for the woman who had been selling corn pods. She had a different story to tell. She said that she never saw the child after we took him to live with us. The father, it appeared, had told everyone that his son was employed as a domestic help, and was not living with him any more. He had been looking for a bride for himself and had left the locality; no one knew where he had gone.

Krishna never returned to the orphanage, and no one saw him afterwards. His father's jhuggi was rented out to someone else.

❧

A month passed. I would think about Krishna, wondering what might have happened to the child. I was constantly praying to God about his well-being. If only I could meet him and see how he was living! I cursed myself every day for sending him away.

Some more time passed and one day, I saw a policeman coming towards my house. He was carrying Krishna on his shoulder, but the child looked pale and very sick. When I opened the door, the policeman laid him down on the carpet and narrated his story. The policeman had found a little child in a semi-conscious state lying on the side of a road. He had picked him up with the intention of taking him to a women and child welfare centre. The child, however, speaking feebly, gave him our address in broken words, and asked to be taken here.

I got a wet towel and wiped Krishna's body before putting him in clean clothes. He looked shrivelled up and so weak that he seemed unable to react to anything. Worried, I called our family doctor to come and see Krishna.

The policeman, meanwhile, told me that the child was most likely working for a begging syndicate and when he had become very ill, they abandoned him and threw him on the street.

I assured the policeman that from now on, we would take care of the child and that he could leave him and go.

'I appreciate your concern and willingness to help, but I cannot leave him with you. I have brought him here because I had an idea about this place, and I took pity on the sick child. But I must take him to a child welfare centre. That's the law.'

I concocted a story and told the policeman that the child was the son of our domestic help who was a widow. She had died a few months ago and there was no one who could take care of the child. So we were keeping him with us. I then told him that he had gotten lost a few days ago, while playing outside the house. It must have been then that he was probably picked up by the child-trafficking mafia. We had been frantically looking for him, and it was a great relief that he had been found and brought back to us.

The policeman was satisfied and left the child with us. He left his telephone number, in case we wanted to send Krishna to a shelter.

In the meantime, the doctor came and upon examining the child, said that he was severely malnourished, dehydrated and had bruises all over his body. He advised me to put him on a liquid diet.

I picked up Krishna and put him in my lap. I tried to make him drink water, but he rejected it. 'If he doesn't drink anything, he has to be taken to the hospital and put on a drip immediately,' said the doctor. It was an emergency. He offered to drive us to his clinic.

I was getting ready to take Krishna to the hospital. He was in my lap. He slowly opened his eyes, looked at me and whispered, 'Ma, you have come.' He tried to lift his hand to touch me, but did not have the strength to do so. His hand dropped down and he became limp and heavy.

'Look at him, Doctor, he does not appear all right!' I shrieked.

The doctor examined him and sighing heavily, said, 'I'm

sorry, he is no more. He has died of dehydration.'

I cried. Why Krishna? Why had he left me? I hugged the child's body close to me and kissed his forehead. I moaned, 'Go to your mother. You'll finally find some peace.'

Since his father had vanished, we performed his last rites.

Krishna had become a passing phase in our lives, but I often thought of him.

After a month or so, his father came to our house in a sober state. We only had the deepest loathing for him. We had no interest in seeing his face; however, we enquired into the purpose of his visit.

He was crying as he spoke, 'God has punished me. I sold my child to the begging mafia. I wanted money for my marriage. First, they cheated me and never gave the amount they had promised. Then my wife, whom I got from Bihar, left me with all the bag and baggage. Now I am left with nothing—no money, no Krishna and no wife. I have come to thank you for performing his last rites.'

He went away. Who knows how much time was left for him to meet the same fate as his wife and son.

The Koh-i-Noor Belongs to Me

It was seven in the evening when Sumita's Air India flight reached the Heathrow airport. She collected her baggage and proceeded towards the gate. While exiting, she saw Wilson waving at her.

'Hi, what brings you here?'

'I had come to drop my wife and my daughters, who are going on a holiday trip. My wife is taking the children of her class for an excursion tour. They will be back after one week.'

Wilson took the bag from Sumita and they started walking towards the taxi stand. He offered to drop her to the hotel where she was booked on the way to his residence. As they reached her place, he suggested taking a final look at the content she had prepared for her presentation, for which she had flown all the way down from Delhi. She agreed.

They sat in her room. He gave a cursory look at the documents she had brought with her and suggested he take them home to read. He then pulled out two cans of beer from the cabinet and gave one to her.

'Before we start our discussion, tell me, are you all right? While you were coming out, I saw you panting for breath. From the time I saw you last, about six months back, you have put on a lot of weight. Jokes apart, you look like a puffed muffin. I wouldn't have recognized you from a distance unless I knew that you were coming. You had to just give me a hint. If you were unwell, I could have easily postponed the meeting.'

'Yes, you're right. I am not too well. Anyway, it's only one week's work left. I can manage. Hopefully, this should be the last hearing before the final verdict. My boss would have sent someone else if I had expressed any reluctance, but I don't want anyone else to take the credit for the hard work already done by me. Politics, you know.'

He again started probing her about her health. 'If you don't mind, you can tell me your problem. I can be of some help. I am well versed with medical jargon. I read a lot of medical literature as a hobby. Many a time, I've felt I should have been in the medical profession, not in the judiciary.'

Sumita was impressed with his sincere and affectionate submission. Although she was not friendly enough with him to open up about her personal life, seeing his confidence and believing in his medical acumen, she started wavering, wondering if she should share her medical issue with him.

A Keralite Christian, Wilson, after graduating from a college in India, studied law at Cambridge University. He now owned his own law firm in London, that too, when he was just in his early fifties. He had married a British school teacher and was naturalized as a Britisher.

He was associated with a law firm in Delhi where Sumita was working as a lawyer. For the ongoing project that had her fly down to London, she was representing an Indian client over a dispute regarding non-performance by a UK-based company. Since, as per the contract, in the event of a dispute, it would have to be settled in London, Sumita had been travelling there to represent her client's case.

Wilson broke the silence, 'Sumita, do you know the meaning of "Mita"? It means a likable person, someone very dear and close to the heart, and "Su" means good. I consider you to be a very dear friend. You are a sumita to me. I do care for you. I am really worried. So do not hesitate. Do share your problem with me. You will feel better. Still, if you don't want to, don't. I respect your privacy.'

He understood her reservation, held her hands affectionately and got up. He took the file she had brought along with him to study at home.

Sumita got up too. She became emotional and in a bid to hide her tears, turned her face away.

'I will come tomorrow to pick you up. We'll head in to the office together. You look tired after the journey. Rest and sleep well.'

He excused himself and quietly went away.

Next morning, Wilson came to Sumita's room one hour before they were scheduled to leave. She was surprised to see him come so early.

'Do we have an early session in the office? I didn't know about it. I have just had my breakfast. Just give me a little time to freshen up and get ready. Would you please wait in the lobby? Or maybe you want to go on ahead? Don't worry, I shall come on my own.'

'No, no, it's nothing of the sort. You see, I couldn't sleep the whole night. I was thinking about you all the time. I was seriously worried. I always remember you as a very good-looking, energetic girl. You are probably just in your mid- or late thirties! What have you done to your body? It appears that you are suffering from some serious problem. Please, tell me. I have purposely come early, to talk to you.'

With his continuous entreaties, Sumita couldn't hide her feelings any more and opened up, 'I have been married for the past ten years and I still haven't been able to conceive. I wasn't worried about this during the first five years of my marriage. Then we started consulting doctors. Since then, all our life and energy has been consumed with visiting fertility clinics, but to no avail. My husband suggested I resign and rest at home. But that would be even more agonizing, thinking only about one thing all the time.'

She proceeded after a short pause, 'My husband is not the blaming kind, but his family keeps on making me feel guilty. Every month, calls keep coming, asking me if I have had my periods. I have told him many times that we should consider adoption, but he is adamant that it be either his own child or no child. He is fixated on the idea that only his biological child can take forward the family name.'

She looked frustrated as she continued, 'Frankly speaking, I am done with the torture and the repeated failures. I have finally told him that no more experimentations. We shall go for surrogacy. Let him have his sperm, and we could use my eggs or anyone else's; at this point, I don't care.'

Wilson thought for a moment and then asked her to get ready, while he waited in the lobby.

To Sumita's surprise, they didn't go to the office, but to some part of London that she was unfamiliar with.

Wilson had taken her to a well-known fertility clinic. Once inside, he asked her to tell the doctor, who was known to him, about her complete history in detail and whether any other treatment would be required.

'It is very difficult to get an appointment so soon but the doctor is a friend of mine, and as a favour, has agreed to talk to you without an appointment. There's no harm in talking, right? Just to get another opinion?' he said.

Sumita had a long conversation with the doctor while Wilson waited outside.

After listening to her case details, the doctor called Wilson inside the room, and discussed her problem further.

According to the doctor, the line of treatment she had been undergoing was perfectly fine. The hormone therapy that she had been getting would have added only 2 to 3 kgs, but this abnormal weight gain was due to something else. Sumita, according to the doctor, was suffering from a stress-induced eating disorder. Her constant guilt over being unable to conceive was the source of immense stress and to compensate for her low self-esteem, she was binge eating.

This was resulting in her abnormal weight gain.

'Moreover, stress is anyway is a big dampener, and comes in the way of getting pregnant,' the doctor remarked.

Wilson thanked him and patted Sumita's back, 'Baby, you are fine. Forget everything. I shall ask my staff to take care of your work. What we'll do today is just relax— partying only, eating, drinking and roaming around the place like nobody's business.'

They laughed and laughed and walked on the London Bridge area hand in hand. Wilson took her to eateries in Mayfair and asked her to order whatever she wanted without feeling guilty. She ate and drank to her heart's content. She had never been so happy for a long, long time; years, in fact. They loitered around the city for the whole day. When they returned to the hotel, it was midnight.

Wilson went along with her up to her room and entered with her, without asking her permission. He bolted the room from inside.

Sumita was beaming with happiness. She had had more than half a bottle of wine and was feeling tipsy. Wilson took her in his arms. She didn't object. He pressed his moist lips and rubbed them against hers. It had an electrifying effect on her. The giddiness gone, she disengaged herself, pushed him and asked him to leave the room at once.

'Sit down. I am not sorry. I am not leaving and I won't apologise either. Let us talk. We need to do some serious talking,' Wilson said in a commanding tone.

He continued, 'See, I have liked you ever since you had come here to work with me two years ago. We were always compatible working partners—that, even you can't deny. I have a suggestion. What about a short fling while you're here? And not because I am forcing it on you, but because we like each other and who knows you get pregnant too.'

Sumita was stunned. She looked straight into his eyes, trying to gauge any ill intention on his part. He appeared to be a very good looking, sober and a perfect gentleman to her. She thought for a moment and surrendered herself to his irresistible charm. She slowly put her arms around him and kissed him on his neck.

Wilson managed to procure week's extension of Sumita's trip on the excuse of winding up the case in its final stage. They were 'honeymooning' and enjoying their interlude to the fullest.

Finally, the time for Sumita's departure had arrived. He escorted her to the airport. They hugged and kissed passionately.

'It is goodbye time. However, I will never be able to forget you, never stop loving you.'

'I don't know what to say. God willing, if I get pregnant, I will inform you and for sure, would quit the job. Even if I don't conceive, I won't be working with your company in the future.'

To avoid any emotional outburst, Wilson joked, 'Better get pregnant. I had been on quite a weighty assignment. You have crushed me to a pulp.'

'You rascal. Shut up,' she laughed loudly.

It was celebration time in Sumita's house. Her husband was bursting with happiness when she announced the news of her pregnancy. She was looking beautiful and radiant. All her relatives and in-laws had gathered in her house. A long list of what is good and what is bad during pregnancy was shared with her. She should stop working, was her mother-in-law's order, which she obediently agreed to follow.

'Thanks for everything. I am quitting the job.' Sumita mailed Wilson.

Time flew and Sumita gave birth to a bonny baby boy, whom she named Arjun.

Arjun, after finishing his engineering from IIT Kanpur, was coming back home. His parents were excited. Seeing his favourite fish fry on the dining table, Arjun remarked, 'I know Papa is allergic to seafood, but for me he still goes personally to buy the best fish available in Delhi. I am so lucky to have parents like you.'

They discussed the next course of action for Arjun. He wanted to do law, whereas his father wanted him to go for an MBA. 'See, there is no sense in doing law now. It will take several years to settle down, whereas you can get employed much sooner."

Arjun ultimately had his say and joined the LLB course in the Delhi University.

One year went by. He surprised his parents by announcing that he had been selected for his summer training course in one of the law firms in London. In fact, out of the many students who had applied, he was the only one who got selected. 'And, I am getting a part-scholarship!'

'Like father like son,' quipped his father. 'Sumi, if you remember I had told you about how I was the only one selected for this job out of so many applicants?'

'By the way, what is the name of that firm?' asked his father.
'Wilson Law Firm.'
'If I remember correctly, this is Sumi's former company!'

Sumita did not comment. This meant that Wilson was keeping a track of his son, she construed.

Arjun did all his three summer training courses from London itself.

After he finished his LLB, he told his mother hesitatingly that even though he didn't want to leave his parents, he had been offered a great position at the same firm where he had been interning over the summer. He also didn't know how to break the news to his father, who was so attached to him. Arjun was certain he wouldn't willingly send him so far away. He wanted his mother to persuade and convince his father, as this could be the opportunity of a lifetime.

Sumita understood what Wilson was up to. He had two daughters and was playing every trick to snatch away Arjun from his parents. She loathed the offer, but seeing her son's obsession for this particular job, she felt helpless.

Finally, his passport and ticket were arranged. It was gloom in the family and soon the time for his departure arrived.

Sumita was sitting on her bed. Her husband was resting in his study. No one had lunch that day. Arjun came and sat quietly near his mother's feet.

'Mummy, London is next door. I'll come whenever you call me. I'll take both of you with me after I get settled. Please take care of Papa. I have no courage to face him. He looks totally shattered.'

Arjun handed over a few blood donation cards to Sumita before leaving for the airport, saying, 'I have been donating blood every year in college. Mine is a rare blood group, as they say. It could be either yours or Papa's. Keep it in case it is needed. You can get in exchange of these cards.'

Sumita's ordeal never seemed to end. She looked at the blood donation slips that Arjun had given. It was disturbing for her to see that Arjun's blood group was different from her and her husband's. She was anxious and hid them away in her closet.

Was it time to tell her husband the truth? What if he chanced upon the cards and suspected something? Tearing them off wouldn't have been wise. She could easily make a story that Arjun's cards were probably changed with someone else's.

All her fears were unfounded, however. With the passage of time, the blood group discrepancy was forgotten; the issue never came to light.

Arjun came home for a fortnight during the Christmas holidays. He looked a very well-groomed and had turned into a handsome young man. His parents were very proud and happy to see him.

'I was unnecessarily worrying about him. Look Sumi, your son has become so good-looking. God is great. We are blessed.'

During his stay, Arjun never stopped praising Wilson, his boss, and the special treatment meted out to him. He was often invited to his house for lunch or dinner. Wilson's daughters were much older than him and usually not around. They were not interested in doing law and led independent lives. However, his wife, after her retirement, would regularly visit her husband's office, helping him in his administrative work. She was an affectionate lady and liked Arjun.

Sumita was bugged to see Arjun's obsession with Wilson. He was either talking about his boss or talking to him on his laptop, most of the time.

'You have come here to meet us, not while away all the time glued to your boss,' Sumita said to him, frustrated.

'Business, Mummy. There are cases for which we have to exchange notes. He is so dependent on me. Even for the slightest of things he asks my opinion. I am so lucky.'

It was getting very clear to Sumita that Wilson had systematically hijacked her son. She suggested to her son that with his parents' advancing age, it was prudent that he should rather be in India with them, and not settle in a foreign land. She felt like talking to Wilson sometime and giving him a piece of her mind. But she could not do any of those things.

One day, while sitting and chatting with his parents, Arjun all of a sudden mentioned the blood donation cards and his rare blood group. He casually asked her about whose blood group matched with his.

Fortunately for Sumita, her husband was not paying attention at the time and had just then got up to take a phone call. Sumita called Arjun in another room and said that she wanted to speak to him about some serious personal matter.

'Now that you are old and mature enough to understand things, I need to tell you something that I have hidden from you and your father. I have been waiting for a long time for this day.' She began,

'When after ten years of our married life, I couldn't conceive, our fertility doctor advised in-vitro fertilization, which means that Papa's sperm and my ovum would be fertilized outside without intercourse and then planted inside my womb. However, unfortunately, when after many trials it was not successful with your father, the doctor suggested for a donor's sperm. That is how you have come into our life. But Papa does not know about this part. He has always been under the impression that it was his sperm.'

Arjun was shocked and found it very hard to take it all in. He asked, 'Who is my biological father?'

'No one knows. That is kept confidential. Even the doctors often do not keep a record. The blood group must be of that of the donor.'

❦

A few years down the line, tragedy struck at Wilson's house. He was diagnosed with advanced- stage cancer. Arjun's work increased manifold.

Within two years, Wilson's condition worsened and there was not much hope given by the doctors. He called Arjun near his bed and spoke slowly, 'Arjun, my son. I am calling you my son because I have always considered you like a son. Please take care of your sisters and your aunty—a gem of a lady. You must run my company as your own. My wife inherits it fully, but I have told her that together, you and she would be in charge.'

After returning from the cortege, Arjun looked for the medical records of Wilson, and found out that his blood group matched his.

He made up his mind and called his mother. 'Mummy, I

have to ask you something. It is a serious matter—in fact, it is a matter of life and death. Just say yes or no. Be fair with me. Please don't lie... is Wilson my biological father?'

'Yes.'

'I am coming to Delhi. We need to talk.'

After Arjun came to Delhi without any prior information, he told his father that Mr Wilson was dead and it would take some time to plan the future strategy. Therefore, he had undertaken that unplanned leave.

He took his father into the study and said that he wanted to share something important about their personal lives, which he had only just recently found out from Sumita.

'Mummy has told me that the fertility clinic where she was taking the treatment actually did fertilize her ovule, not with yours but with a donor sperm, without your knowledge, lest you may get hurt. Therefore, my biological father is someone anonymous and whose identity has been kept confidential. But I don't care. I have only known you as my father. I love and respect both, you and mummy, more than ever before.'

Arjun's father, obviously shocked in the beginning, slowly overcame his emotions, became composed and declared, 'I would have been much happier if Sumi told me all this before. I am not a petty-minded person. Sumi has not done any wrong, there was no need to hide this from me. As a matter of fact, may God bless the donor. He gave me a son like you. You are a Koh-i-Noor and the fact is that the Koh-i-Noor belongs to me, and only me. And it is where it should be.'

The Honey Trap?

Nisha picked up the invitation card from the dining table, which her son Praveen had placed a little while ago. It was an invite to Praveen's secretary Raveena's wedding. Praveen's twin sister Priya glanced at the card, and said, 'The date of the wedding is that of today and Praveen hasn't said anything about it, which means buddy has no plans to go. Strange, isn't it?'

Nisha had been observing that her son was in a sombre mood for the past few days, which was quite unlike him. She knew very well that Praveen would eventually share what was on his mind soon, so she told Priya not to bug him.

Praveen soon sat at the dining table with Priya, while

Nisha went inside to arrange for tea and snacks. When Praveen saw the questioning look on his sister's face he said that he was not going to the wedding. Priya didn't probe further.

However, Praveen started speaking after his mother brought the refreshments and all three were having their grub. 'I got this invite a week back, but it was lying in the office. There is something that I would now like to share with you both.'

He explained, 'Raveena came with this card to the office a week ago, a little late when most of the staff had left and I was winding up. She requested me to sit as she wanted to talk about something very important.'

'She began, "Sir, the atmosphere in my house is vicious, very hostile. My elder brother who is making all the arrangements is complaining all the time about expenses. They have taken all my deposits, spent it on my trousseau and now crying foul about paucity of funds. Sir, you don't know, what is poverty, what does marriage of a daughter means in a deprived family. How I hate being poor and having to think about money all the time. I wish I wasn't born. There is no pleasure for me." And she started sobbing.

'I tried to console her, by saying that things would get alright after she would get married and start a new life with her husband, the person of her choice.'

"I wish that were true," she replied. "As a matter of fact, that is also not the case. I don't like that man. He has no class. He is my parents' choice. He tries to speak in English all the time to impress me, but doesn't know the language. Whenever I see him, I start comparing him with you—your mannerisms, your diction, your sophistication and your grooming, and I get depressed. Whenever he tries to touch me, I am repulsed and fantasize about you instead. To make matters worse, he is not earning well, doing some average kind of job, and has a big family. I have forced him to rent at least a one-bedroom flat for us only, which fortunately he has agreed to do."

'I felt uncomfortable in her company and as the office was almost empty and the guard and the driver were waiting for us to leave. I got up from my chair, made a move to leave and told her to have faith in God, things would get all right.

'What she said next was most unexpected, "Sir, you are not yet married. Please marry me. You don't know, but you are on my mind all the time. I am madly in love with you. I adore you. I worship you and I swear if you marry me I'll prove to be the best wife in the world. I will serve your mother like a maid. Say yes and I will stop this stupid drama. Please say yes. I want a commitment now."'

'She suddenly got up from her chair, came behind me, while I was standing, and hugged me from the back. And to make matters worse, just then my driver came to collect my bag, saw us, and quickly closed the door and left.'

'It was embarrassing for me. I sternly ordered her to go back to her seat and told her to stop that nonsense, and reminded her that she was a good fifteen plus years younger to me. I had, in fact, never given any indication to her of such a feeling from my side.'

'Take this out of your mind. Don't marry the man if you don't want to. You are only twenty-five. What is the hurry to marry? You are employed, earning. Wait till you find someone of your liking and then marry. Go now. I have to also leave.'

'I left the card there and went out. She also went sobbing.'

Nisha and Priya, who were intently listening to Praveen, were left shell-shocked.

Nisha said, 'See, Praveen you have already crossed forty, and not married. With two aborted affairs, first when you turned down the offer, saying you were not ready to get married and then that Tamilian Doctor Shubha, a very nice girl whom you were courting for more than five years, left you for her mother's brother, with whom she was betrothed as a child, out of parental pressure. Since the past two years we have been looking for a girl for you but in vain. Nothing seems to materialize. You are also not taking interest. In case you like Raveena, I'll ask for her hand and get you married to her.'

Priya retorted, 'What are you saying, Mummy? You have not seen the girl, I have met that shit of a girl once. She is nothing to look at, dark-skinned, and hails from a lower middle class background. And to camouflage her average looks, she flaunts her sexuality overtly. Her body language, her demeanour, the way she looks seductively at every male, from a clerk to seniors in the office, she is by no means worthy of our family and status.'

'OK I agree, but suppose on Praveen's advice she cancels her wedding? We can groom her. She will improve after she comes here and gets our love,' Nisha remarked.

Praveen intercepted, 'Please, both of you, just stop it. I am not going to marry her. She may marry anyone or remain unmarried. I don't care. I don't want any scandal in the office. As it is, the driver has seen her hugging me. I am worried.'

Suddenly, Nisha put Praveen's phone on the speaker and dialled Raveena's home. When Raveena's mother answered the phone, Nisha asked, 'Is Raveena's wedding today?' After getting a reply in the affirmative, she said that she rang up to excuse herself and her son for their inability to attend the wedding.

'Now you know that the wedding is not called off,' Priya said. 'I am sure it was all a big emotional drama to entice my brother. She is a big opportunist, an ambitious person.' Priya after a while suggested to her brother, 'Bro, my advice is that you terminate Raveena's services immediately. She is preposterously a dangerous element. She would ruin your career; make you the butt of a joke. You are in such a senior position. Don't play with your future.'

Praveen laughed and said, 'I am neither a novice, nor a child. I can handle the situation. This is Raveena's first job, she is immature and childish. She was recommended by my bosses, as they wanted to oblige someone. It won't be easy to dismiss her. With passage of time, she would learn to behave, no problem. Only, I shall be more careful.'

Nisha had lost her husband, a colonel in the Indian army, while he was fighting terrorists in Jammu and Kashmir. Praveen and Priya were only fifteen then. She had brought them up with extreme courage and dignity. She also took her children with her to receive the gallantry award given to her husband posthumously to make them feel proud of their father. She never cried before her children and told them that most army person's wives prepare themselves to become a widow, some time in their lifetime right after they get married. She told them that she never regretted marrying a person trained in combat fighting, and hers was a love marriage.

Nisha was teaching in the Army Public School at the time when the tragedy struck them. Many army wives pick up some kind of a job, so that they learn to manage independently both the house and children during long spells of nonfamily station postings of their husbands.

It was much easier to bring up Priya, without her father, and Nisha got her happily married at an appropriate time into a known family and with a boy of her liking. However, it was difficult to bring up the adolescent Praveen. His personality changed after the tragedy. Suddenly from an outgoing and jovial teenager, he turned into an introvert. He also became extra protective and possessive of his mother. He declared that he would never leave his mother and any girl who would marry him would be told in advance that she should never talk of any separate establishment. He even refused to go abroad for education or job for this reason.

Raveena joined the office after one month's leave. She had mellowed down a bit and immersed herself in her work completely. Praveen was much relieved. He never asked about her relationship with her husband and she also avoided the topic.

A few months passed. Out of the blue, Raveena declared that she wanted to share some urgent matter with Praveen.

'Say quickly whatever it is that you have to say, no melodrama please, as this is office.'

'I wish I could show you marks of beating by my husband on my torso. He never beats me on my face, to avoid getting any kind of sympathy and attention from my colleagues. The physical and mental torture meted out to me at regular intervals is becoming unbearable. The bone of contention is money. He takes all my salary, and gives me just enough money for commuting and petty expenses.'

She added, 'Sir, you were right, I should not have married him, but my elder brother, a devilish person, wanted to throw me out of the house before his own wedding, which took place shortly after mine. It never occurred to me that I could have left the house and started living separately in a women's hostel, and not listened to my brother.'

Praveen advised her to open a bank account near the office, not in the knowledge of her husband and start depositing some amount there before taking her salary home. He promised to help her in getting an account opened in her single name, as he knew the bank manager very well. He also warned her not to discuss her personal life with him or with anyone else in the office, or else she would be thrown out of her job.

The very next day, Raveena opened an account close to the office with an initial deposit of 1,000 rupees given by Praveen, however, he never shared this information with his mother or sister.

In order to get attention from Praveen, Raveena changed her strategy: she stopped complaining about her family life, instead started playing mind games with him by bitching about their colleagues. Praveen was enjoying the gossip and even started encouraging her. Gradually she became the apple of his eye and an eyesore for the rest of the staff. Any member of the staff who would offend her would get a drubbing from the boss. They were engaged in a bitching game usually after office hours and it soon became a regular practice that Praveen would drop her at a metro station on his way back home. Often as a gesture of camaraderie they would hold each others' hands while gossiping. Slowly, the indiscipline and favouritism going on in his office reached the owners, who told Praveen to ask for Raveena's resignation or else they would serve her a termination notice which would not be in the interest of her future job prospects. Thus, Raveena was made to resign.

Praveen, however informed his family that she left because she got a better job. No guessing, Priya was much relieved, thinking it was good riddance to bad rubbish.

※

Nisha started pestering Praveen that it was time he got married and start a family otherwise loose character girls like Raveena would keep coming into his life to entice him and take advantage of him. Moreover, their relatives had started talking about his single status, and name calling him to be a non-marrying kinds, to his mother's great embarrassment. Praveen did not care less about family gossip but relented.

So talks began at a slower pace, it was rejection either from the boy's side or the girl's on some pretext or the other. Finally, they decided to lower the bar set for the selection of matches. But Praveen didn't want to compromise too much and was ready to wait.

A few of Nisha's relatives were settled in the US and have been requesting her to visit them for long. Praveen suggested that his mother take a trip abroad and spend some time with her kin and resume the bride hunting exercise after some time. Nisha agreed, and left on a two month's leave.

The very next day of Nisha's exit, Praveen was surprised to see Raveena at his door late in the evening. She told him to call his mother as she wanted to talk to her. After learning that she had left for the US, she requested to speak to his sister. On being told that she lived with her family in her own house, Raveena started crying. Praveen got worried and asked her to come in. Reluctantly she followed him inside his house.

Praveen fetched her a glass of water and made her sit down in the drawing room. She said, 'After I was thrown out of your office, I got a part-time job in a travel agency, on a meagre salary. My husband was also on a low paid job. The house rent and the expenses were getting too much to bear. Fortunately, my husband has got a job in Dubai through some agent and has already left. In the starting few months, he has to pay back the loan he had taken from the agent, and then would send money to me. I have come here to ask for some help to sail through in the meantime.'

Praveen wanted to seek Priya's advice, but it was late, so he asked Raveena how much she wanted. She requested him to let her stay in the night as it was risky to return at this late hour. She promised to leave in the morning.

Praveen told her that she could sleep in the guest room and asked her if she wanted to eat something before retiring for the day. He also told her to help herself. They finally ate something and then retired to their separate rooms.

Raveena had brought a bag with her, which her husband had helped her pack. She changed into a designer lingerie and a see-through sheer nighty that her husband had given her a few days back. She tiptoed towards Praveen's room and then slowly went inside his room and sat on his bed near his feet. Praveen understood her intentions and gave in. She won.

❦

Raveena kept visiting Praveen for the next few days. Whenever Priya tried to contact her brother she was told that he usually came very late in the evening so was unavailable. She got worried and decided to go in the daytime in his absence.

When she entered the house she was shocked to find a few ladies undergarments hanging in Praveen's bathroom,

The Honey Trap?

and learnt from the maid about a woman coming in the house in the evenings and staying till morning, since their mother left. She decided to confront her brother. Next day early in the morning she barged into the house, and to her horror found Raveena and Praveen having their breakfast together.

Raveena, smilingly greeted Priya and got up from her seat. She gave a pat on Praveen's shoulder, a peck on his cheek, then bade him goodbye and left.

'What is this?' fumed Priya.

Praveen replied, 'Sit down and listen.' He apprised Priya about the story Raveena had told him, and also that she had only come to ask for some monetary help.

'Don't fool me. You are being honey trapped, which you must have realized by now.'

'OK if you insist, she is my mistress. It is consensual. This arrangement is a quid pro quo. She needs money; I need her services.'

'Disgusting.' Priya couldn't take it any more, and got up to leave. 'I am going to tell Mummy everything.'

He said in a commanding tone, 'Sit down and let me finish before you go. I am sure you know that Shubha also came here to spend a few nights with me, and Mummy approved. What do you think? I didn't spend anything on her? I took her to the best eateries and gave her expensive gifts. Finally, she left me. The only difference is that she was my girlfriend and poor Raveena is my mistress.'

He continued, 'Sis, I advise you not to bother Mummy now. Let her come back. With Raveena, there is no commitment, no pregnancy, no baggage for me. Shubha broke my heart, I went into depression. Raveena won't.'

Priya was dumbfounded. While leaving, she yelled, 'I'll never come back in this house till that prostitute is visiting you!'

Priya thought about the matter and ultimately decided not to say anything to Nisha. She did not want her to face embarrassment from her relatives, in case she decided to share her agony with them.

However, she was not convinced with the story that Raveena had told to her brother. She hired a detective agency and tasked them to shadow Raveena.

After a week, the truth emerged. Raveena's husband was not in Dubai, but very much living in the city and working in a printer's shop on a meagre salary. The general impression of the man in his neighbourhood was that he was a recluse. Raveena was employed in a travel agency on a part-time basis.

Their neighbours said that she was working in a call centre on night shifts.

She told everything to her brother, and also about the husband pimping his wife. Praveen couldn't care less whether the husband went to Dubai or not, or used his wife as a honey trap.

'I am not surprised. Possibly, he is an accomplice and engaged in pimping his wife. However, I am not bothered. Both of us are having a good time. That is what matters,' reacted Praveen.

Nisha was shocked to hear of her son's depravity after she returned. She ordered him to break all kinds of contact with Raveena, including telephoning her, which Praveen did. Nisha postponed her matchmaking exercise, to let things settle down, fearing that a scandal could break out, spoiling the reputation of her family.

After a year or so, Nisha received an offer from a girl's side, whom they had previously rejected on account of her average looks. Praveen would do anything to please his mother, so gave a go-ahead and both him and the girl started spending time together in order to know each other better. Praveen was impressed with her pleasant disposition, her cultured behaviour and agreed to marry her. Nisha breathed a sigh of relief and a brief engagement ceremony was performed soon after.

Nisha wanted an early marriage and invited the girl's parents to discuss the matter. A date within one month of the engagement was fixed and both families started preparations on a war footing.

꙰

Alas, the happiness was short-lived. Just a day before the wedding, Praveen's would be father-in-law came with a few of his relatives and started abusing Nisha's family.

'How dare you hide such a thing about him? We are told that Praveen was having a mistress for a long time and has even secretly married her.'

'Yes, he had a girlfriend, but is not married to her. She is happily married with a husband and a child. It was a case of brief infatuation that ended long ago.' Nisha tried to explain.

However, it was all in vain. The girl's father had already decided to cancel the marriage. Nisha was greatly anguished and suffered a nervous breakdown. Praveen felt very guilty and ashamed of what he had done to his mother. Priya suspected

Raveena's hand in the fiasco; however, it was never confirmed.

※

With the passage of time, things started getting back to normal. Nisha worried a great deal about Praveen and his future. She pondered over the possibilities and arrived at a decision. She called Praveen and told him about her plan. After all, he had to settle down in life. Things couldn't go on like that. Praveen loved his mother very much and therefore agreed to abide by whatever his mother would ask him to do.

Nisha told Praveen to call Raveena, as she wanted to talk to her. She requested Raveena to divorce her husband and marry her son. Raveena was very happy to hear that. As an ambitions person, she always wanted to lead the life of a well-to-do woman. She replied that she always loved Praveen and did not love her husband.

She also promised to talk to her husband, but laid down one condition that she would fight for the custody of her five-year-old son, who would have to be adopted by Praveen with all his rights.

Raveena's husband had come to realize that his wife was double-crossing him. However, despite his anger, he agreed for divorce, but with two conditions: all expenses of the proceedings would be borne by Nisha and he wouldn't give his son's custody to his wife. When the judge asked the child as to where would he like to stay after his parents' separation, he flatly refused to go with his mother and opted to go with his father. Raveena was stripped even of visiting rights, as her husband proclaimed that a bad character woman would be a bad influence in the growing years of the child.

It took one year for the divorce to take place with mutual consent. As a parting gift, the estranged husband requested Nisha to deposit a good amount of money on long term basis, which would take care of his son's higher education. Nisha obliged.

❧

It was an eventful day for Nisha for two reasons. One, it was Praveen's fiftieth birthday and two, it was also his wedding day.

The wedding was to take place in the registrar's office on the same very day, which was prefixed. After which, the couple were to proceed for their honeymoon. Praveen had booked a suite in some resort in Manesar.

❧

Priya understood very well under what circumstances her

mother took the decision. She must have weighed both pros & cons of taking Raveena, a girl of much disrepute, as her daughter-in-law, but probably it was the only option left to her. She decided to give company to her mother.

When Priya entered the house to look for her mother, it was dusk, but the lights were not on. Priya knew, whenever her mother was in a pensive mood, she would sit in a dark corner alone, contemplating about the flow of happenings in her life. Priya put her arms around her shoulders and closed on her cheeks with hers. They were wet. Nisha was crying. Is this what she had wanted for her son? She remembered her husband like never before. Praveen was a very handsome, brilliant lad that the colonel was extremely proud of.

'Mummy please don't cry.'

'I am not crying, don't worry. I'll be all right. I see a silver lining. Raveena is still young. She will bear me my grandchildren to play with. I am a fatalist, maybe it was all predestined. I have no regrets.'

Nisha held her daughter's hand and both of them went out to have dinner in a posh restaurant to celebrate the marriage that was taking place in their family, albeit in their absence. It was evident that Nisha would forgive her son eventually, but whether Priya would ever be able to love and respect her sister-in-law remained to be seen.

Acknowledgments

My father's small library, which had a good collection of fiction and non-fiction, both in Hindi and English, gave me ample opportunity of reading and learning at home. Therefore, the primary acknowledgment goes to my late father, who instilled reading habits in his children from an early age.

I owe heartfelt thanks to many people who have not only encouraged me but given valuable suggestions. Gaurav Bhatara, a spiritually-inclined, law professional whose inputs to cover up my naivety in legal matters was critical. My academician daughter, Surabhi Aggarwal, for insightful advice on issues related to sociology and psychology. My cousins Neerja and Pradeep, who were always ready with critical comments. I am also grateful to my publishers—Rupa Publications India—for taking a chance on me.

Last but not the least my husband, who has been a constant source of inspiration.